Heart's Blood

The Crown of the Queen

Two stories from The Twelve Kingdoms and The Uncharted Realms

by Jeffe Kennedy

Thank you for reading!

Credits
Content Editor: Deborah Nemeth (Heart's Blood); Peter Senftleben (The Crown of the Queen)
Line and Copy Editor: Rebecca Cremonese (The Crown of the Queen)
Back Cover Copy: Erin Nelson Parekh (The Crown of the Queen)
Cover Design: Louisa Gallie

Table of Contents

Heart's Blood   1

The Crown of the Queen   95

HEART'S BLOOD

A Story of the Twelve Kingdoms

by Jeffe Kennedy

A dark fairytale retelling of a princess robbed of rank, husband and even her name. Nix is nothing. The Princess Natilde—her former waiting woman—attacked her on the journey to wed Prince Cavan, stripping her of everything and taking her place. With no serving skills, Nix becomes a goose girl. Perhaps if Nix keeps her promise never to reveal who she really is, Natilde won't carry out her vile threats. Prince Cavan entered his arranged marriage determined to have a congenial, if not loving relationship with his future queen—for the sake of both their kingdoms. But, his wife repels him more each day and he finds himself absurdly drawn to the lovely Nix. With broken vows, anguish and dark secrets between them, Cavan and Nix struggle to find the magic to restore what's gone terribly wrong…if it ever can be.

Warning: This story contains a graphic sexual assault scene and the beheading of a magical horse (this is part of the original fairytale and takes place off the page).

~ 1 ~

E VEN THE GRAY crystals sleeting down contributed to the dinginess of the day. The old snow of the inner courtyard, scuffed by the passage of many feet, lay in stripes of darkest mud crossing the drifts of iron-toned ice, absorbing the dismal new snowfall without a sign of change.

The new arrivals—Cavan couldn't quite think of the woman as his bride, not yet, though the vows had been said and sealed—showed their relief at reaching the castle in the lines of their sagging shoulders, their hurried movements as they dismounted. Astonishing that she had journeyed to Marcellum with only a waiting woman for company. But then, rumor had Old Queen Isyn of the Remus Isles eccentric in more ways than that. She'd sent a ship to carry her daughter, Natilde, to the shores of Erie, and promised protection she'd sent with the princess would see her arrive safely.

Cavan had assumed that meant an actual guard, but apparently not.

He'd stayed back instead of greeting this Natilde personally, needing those moments to process his first impressions of her without guarding his true reaction. A moment of honesty with himself, even if he must forever hide it after this. He'd liked her letters, but people were not always the same in person as in their writing. As if feeling his gaze, the dark haired woman looked up, scanning the tower and fixing on the window where he stood. Out of long habit, though she could hardly see him clearly, he shuttered his expression, the moment of honesty already over.

"What do you think?" His father laid a hand on his shoulder.

"Does it matter?" Cavan bled the bitterness from his voice before it could snake in, keeping it smooth, courtly. All any king could wish of his heir. "I've made my vows and will keep them."

"She seems to be as beautiful as promised. That will help."

"All cats are gray in the dark."

King Wyn made a disapproving sound. "You'll find yourself out of bed more than in it. In time you'll appreciate at least a pleasant visage to look upon. Her beauty will do credit to the throne of Erie."

The woman—Natilde, he reminded himself—tilted her head and, with a wry curve of her reddened lips, sank into a curtsy. He lifted a hand in acknowledgement, feeling nothing but a vague dread at the sight of her. He'd known better than to expect any kind of instant affection, but he had hoped, in the cynical way one looked forward to distant spring, to be at least attracted. Like a stallion bred to a mare, he had little choice in this pairing. He envied the horses in this moment, subject only to their basest urges, not requiring more than that to breed and be done.

He supposed he didn't require more either. But glimpsing the potential for affection might have helped. Of course, the horses wouldn't be spending the rest of their lives together, either.

"Regard grows over time." his father squeezed his shoulder. "Complete the alliance, get an heir, then dally with all the maids you like."

Not something Cavan would ever do. Vows were meant to

be kept, not discarded at whim or convenience. He'd seen enough of how his father's dallying had wounded his mother, weakening the marriage and her, until she finally slipped into poor health, then death. Cavan steeled himself to keep his promises, do his duty by the throne—and hardened his instinctive flinch at that vision of the future. Below, servants escorted Natilde inside the great doors, taking her to the bridal chamber where they would put the final seal on their marriage before the sun rose again.

Conducted long-distance and bloodlessly, the rites that bound them to each other had been as cold as the flat sky. No reason this final coming together should be any different. Or so Cavan had tried to resign himself, his heart as bleak and gray as the endless winter. He'd seen the model with other kings and queens, with their carefully formal, soulless marriages, and all his life had known better than to expect more.

And yet, some part of him had hoped regardless.

He should go and get it done with, but instead he lingered at the window, though delay and denial would change nothing. Telling himself the tableau fascinated him, he observed as the waiting woman, head bowed, stopped a groom from taking one of the horses. She slipped a pale hand, transparent ice like the snow around her, along the mare's fine-boned jaw. Inclining her head, she seemed to speak to the horse, then nodded as if hearing a reply.

He smiled a little at it, feeling the crack in the stone of his own face. Not at her speaking to the horse—he did that with his own steeds, as many good horsemen did—but that she fancied the animal could answer. Superstitious. Perhaps peasant stock, given her rough garb, with their many uneducated beliefs. But enviable in her simplicity, her childlike affection for the horse.

Something he'd long left behind. Pitiful. Envying first his own stallion, then a waiting woman.

"I suppose we'll have to find a place for her." His father looked out also. "We can hardly send her home immediately. I have no ships to spare or guard to take her back to the port."

"Princess Natilde will no doubt wish to have a familiar servant. I'll inquire."

"Do so. And, take my advice, delay no longer. Starting your marriage with the insult of apparent reluctance will only poison things between you." The king sighed, a rare sound of regret, and clasped him on the shoulder again. Squeezed and met his gaze, eyes paler than the gray snow. "I know this isn't easy and you are strangers, but perhaps you will find that you enjoy one another."

Despite the steadiness of the king's assurance, doubt crept through his tone like the feathers of frost threading across the window pane as the sun set in midwinter haste.

Taking hold of himself, Cavan turned from the scene below and went to meet his bride.

NATILDE INDULGED ONE moment longer in the silken texture of Falada's hide, the sweet, hay-scented breath washing warmly over her as the horse murmured words of encouragement. At least, now that they'd arrived, she could talk with Falada again, as long as no one overheard them. A small happiness, but she suspected she would subsist on a similar diet of scant crumbs of pleasure for the rest of her life. And be grateful to have that much. At least they'd lived to reach the castle.

"If your mother only knew," Falada muttered, "her heart

would break."

"One reason she can't ever know. She cannot help me, not without our kingdoms going to war. I'll find a place here and it will be fine. I never needed to be queen. Or wife to a man I've never met."

"It's who you are, wanted or not." The mare gnashed over the words with her blunt teeth. "Not that viper's, who even now beds your lawful husband."

"Not mine. Never mine. Not now." The sullen gray castle walls rose around her, a deeper shade than the empty sky that shed gritty snow, pricking her cold cheeks. "He belongs to Princess Natilde and I am no longer her. I am no one now, and there is freedom in that."

"Unless she's discovered."

"She won't be. Remember I vowed never to tell, and guaranteed your silence also."

"An oath made under duress carries no weight."

"This one does. She won't hesitate to carry out her threats. You saw—." She broke off, unwilling to admit the images to her mind of what had happened. How she'd promised and groveled, just to have it come to an end. That Falada had witnessed her violation and degradation only made it worse.

Falada nuzzled her in comfort. "It grieves me that I couldn't stop it. If I could trade this horse's body and have my magic again, I would."

"You made the choice for good reasons. And came with me to be my companion, not my protector. The talisman Mother gave me should have—" The illness of terror rose up, choking her. That, too, had been easily wrested from her. "No. I'll keep to my word and so will you. Tell no one our secret. In truth, better not to talk at all—the people here…they won't understand. Erie and the Twelve have been so long without magic, none of them believe in it anymore. And she will kill you if you tell. I can't lose you along with everything else."

The horse shook her head in irritation as the groom returned, laying a hand to her bridle. "Beggin' your pardon, miss, but I'd best get this one stabled."

She took his measure. Stocky, coarse-featured but with gentle hands. "This one is Falada. Treat her with care as she's of rare and fine breeding."

"Aye, miss." He ducked his head at her, clucked to Falada and led her away, leaving Natilde standing alone in the yard, uncertain what to do with herself. How did servants know where to go?

"Well, come inside then," a woman called from a side doorway, one wafting smoke-tinged steam. The kitchens, no doubt. "The Princess says you've not many skills and you're not needed to attend her." The woman sized her up as she approached. "Prince Cavan says to find you a place."

The woman pulled the door shut behind her, the kitchens thankfully warmer and considerably brighter than the frozen yard. "I'm Brenna Crocker, housekeeper and thus head of all the servants. What do they call you?"

Taken aback, Natilde had no immediate answer. Not her own name, as that had been stripped from her along with her clothes, dignity, pride and rank. Innocence. Leaving only self-loathing behind. She could not take the viper's name as her own, no more than she'd wrap herself in the discarded skin of a snake.

"You speak Common Tongue, don't you?" Mrs. Crocker spoke more slowly, enunciating the words. Then frowned at her. "Not a mute or an idiot, are ye?"

For a long moment, she considered it. Play mute. Be the

idiot without fully formed thoughts and she'd never be expected to answer questions, a barrier against accidentally speaking of what had happened and bringing down the promised wrath. Easier, especially given how the sudden, intense tumble to her current status had left her battered in some crushing unnamable way. *If your mother only knew, her heart would break.* But her mother wouldn't know. The promised magic, her mother's protection had shredded as easily as the delicate silk of her undergarments under the claws and knife of the vicious waiting woman. Reducing her to nothing.

But pretending to idiocy would be the coward's way and she'd already been too much of that.

"Nix," she breathed. Then spoke it louder, laying claim to it, the nothingness that remained her one belonging. They would belong to each other, her and the empty space. Better to embrace it, the final end of her tentative dreams and the grander ones her mother had nursed for her.

Mrs. Crocker wiped her mouth with the back of a coal-stained hand. "Can't say as I think much of your mother, laying that fate upon you with such a name. But so be it, Nix. Sit with some tea and tell me what you know how to do. We'll find a place for you."

~ 2 ~

N ATILDE'S DARK BEAUTY matched the bridal chamber perfectly, as if she—or her people—had somehow known and planned for it. An absurd notion, that her appearance could have been engineered. And yet, her crimson-painted lips matched the brocade spread, her glossy chestnut hair an echo of the carved wooden bed posts, the ice green of her eyes shades lighter than the malachite tiles of the fireplace she posed in front of. Striking, indeed, but somehow not at all pleasant to look upon.

That glittering gaze drank him in as he approached, with all the ardent hunger any man would wish for from his wife. Yet something in the avaricious edge of it curdled his gut, a sense of illness Cavan bore down on. He'd bedded women before and she would be no better or worse than they, royal blood or not. *All cats are gray in the dark.* His men bantered that one about, that phrase he'd unwisely lobbed back at his father, though the king had let it pass. Douse the candles and one woman would be the same as the next. Maidservant, peasant wench or virgin bride. All the same betwixt their thighs.

"My prince." Natilde curtseyed as she had in the courtyard, with studied grace and a sultry pout. "I'm gratified to see your handsomeness and royal mien were most accurately reflected in

12

your portrait."

"I'm afraid you have the advantage of me, my lady." He lifted her hand and brushed a kiss over the back of it, vaguely unsettled by the scent of her perfumed flesh, as heavily floral as the brocaded bed curtains. Of course, she'd traveled many days and likely wished to cover the odors of her journey. A thought that did nothing to appease his distaste. "I never received a likeness of you."

"My mother, Queen Isyn, does not believe in such things." Natilde gave him a conspiratorial smile that oddly made him like her less. "You've no doubt heard the rumors."

"No?" He made it a question, to invite her to confide more, though of course he had heard bits and bits. If nothing else, the king's spies had gathered all they could—innuendo or other-wise—about their potential new ally. Which wasn't much. The people of the Isles of Remus had always been insular. Far enough off the coast and scattered enough to make conquest difficult, the Queen Isyn's kingdom had evaded being drawn under High King Uorsin's rule.

With Queen Isyn failing and his marriage to Natilde, he'd be king of both lands eventually. It paid to know what that would mean. Wild tales of witchcraft, sorcery and faeries obscured the picture more than a bit.

"Paintings steal the soul, didn't you know?" Her green eyes caressed him with feline glee, daring him to fall for her bait. "Which means I hold yours, a tighter bond than any wedding vows your priests could tie us with."

The hair raising on the back of his neck, he released her hand and stepped back. "The marriage is not yet consummated."

She clasped her hands together and held them between her breasts, drawing his gaze to her generously displayed bosom. He tried to savor the sight, to prime himself for his duty. He needed be looking for reasons to like her, not the reverse. "A jest only!" She laughed gaily. "I meant to tease, my prince. Don't let a sour old woman's superstitious beliefs color what should be a passionate new beginning for us."

"Have you no affection for your mother then?"

A sneer rippled over her lovely face, wrenching it into a flash of ugliness, quickly banished with a pretty smile. "I am glad to be away from her and her provincial islands. I shall be a far greater, more powerful queen than she could ever hope to be."

"My father continues hale and hearty," he warned her. "You will remain a princess for some time yet."

"A status that suits me exceedingly well." She closed the distance between them and stroked his cheek, almost as he'd check the soundness of the hocks in a horse he meant to buy. "Husband," she added, in a tone of satisfaction.

"Not entirely," he said, unsettled by the prick of his instincts, warning him to escape. "Not yet."

"Then, by all means…" She smiled, her red mouth seductive in the firelight. "Let's put that to rights, as we both *vowed* to do."

The reminder pricked him. He had so vowed, and he would see it through. "I'll call your serving woman to tend you."

"No." As if realizing she'd sounded sharp, Natilde stroked his cheek, her nails a scrape of omen, and gave a rueful shake of her head. "She is a coarse, useless thing, recruited for this journey only because no one else wished to travel so far from home. More superstition. I suspect she lied and falsified her references. She might not even be from Remus. I'd prefer another servant. Surely anyone you have will be far better."

"I shall see to it then." He moved away from her with a sense of reprieve. One he shouldn't cling to. "I'll see that a bath is prepared for you and then shall return later."

Her face hardened slightly. Insulted, perhaps. So be it. He'd yet to feel any stirrings of lust for her that would enable him to bed her as duty and his vows required. Ridding her of the heavy perfume could only help.

"You could stay," she pouted, though her simmering ire rendered it less effective. "Assist me yourself."

"I'm a prince," he told her, "not a bath servant. Speaking of which—how shall we occupy your former waiting woman?"

"Send her away."

He raised a brow at her callousness to the companion of her long journey. "It is winter, my lady, and a harsh one. Your isles are gentle in climate, but not so this far inland. She would likely not survive, were we to turn her out. At best she'd fall to an unwelcome fate."

Rather than abashed, Natilde seemed pleased at the prospect and waved a hand. "I care not, but I can understand such a thing might reflect poorly on you. I bend to your will, husband. Whatever you find to occupy her, it must be simple. She is a low thing."

"Understood." With that, he stepped into the cooler, cleaner air of the hall.

And wondered how he'd force himself to go back in again.

NIX KNEW HOW to do many things. She could dance and speak several languages, able to make charming conversation in all of them with diplomatic skill. She rode with a perfect seat, understood how to feed a village, the political status of all the known kingdoms—the Twelve, Kooncelund and beyond—along with who stood to be an ally or an enemy. Not to mention all those small spells to please and divert the faeries, to ensure continued good luck. Nothing like her mother's sorcery. She'd never managed that, something of a disappointment in that arena. Which made her all the better to be sent off to be a foreign bride.

She'd trained to be a queen—skills not at all useful in a servant.

Under Mrs. Crocker's gentle, but insistent questioning, Nix found herself as wanting as the housekeeper clearly did. She dared not risk revealing her true nature. Couldn't even contemplate what Natilde would visit upon her. Not again. To protect Falada and herself, she must be forever nothing more than the serving maid she appeared to be. One who'd somehow never done a useful chore in her life.

"You cannot cook or sew," Mrs. Crocker recapped with some exasperation. "You've never done laundry, scrubbed a floor or served at dinner. What on earth did you do at your previous home?"

Flailing for an answer, she cast about the warm kitchen, empty of other servants in this lull before supper preparation, hoping for inspiration. Then gasped aloud when her gaze fell on Prince Cavan, darkly imposing, standing in the doorway and staring hard at her, anger in the line of his jaw.

For a panicked moment, she imagined he'd somehow found her out and, flinging herself back in an instinctive need to hide, she nearly toppled over the rude bench, saved only by the rung she'd tucked her feet behind, scraping her shins painfully. Mrs. Crocker followed the direction of her gaze, but seemed unsurprised to see the prince standing there. Or, rather, not taken aback by it.

"Your Highness," she nodded, but did not rise. "What can I do for you that you could not send for?"

His gaze lingered over Nix, taking her measure in a way she recognized, a way she herself had been taught, to weigh the value of a person, their relative worth and usefulness. But with no glimmer of any other knowledge. He believed her a servant, which meant Natilde would have no reason to make good her threats. Easing her breath, she watched him through her lashes. She'd spotted him before, standing in the tower window, warm light framing his lean body, face shadowed. This close, he looked no less brooding, body lean and lethal as the sword he was reputed to wield so well, gray eyes like granite framed by lashes as black as his coal-dark hair. For his part, he looked away, dismissing her as beneath further notice and turning his attention to the housekeeper.

"My bride requires a maid or two to assist her. I'm sure you know the best choices. Send whoever you choose up along with a hot bath, soap and so forth. Anything she requests, of course." His words, all graciously chosen, nevertheless seemed barbed with displeasure.

"Of course, Your Highness." Mrs. Crocker folded her hands around her tea cup. "And for you?"

He hesitated, an almost palpable pause that tempted Nix to glance up, though she managed to tame the impulse. "Have you any of that Branlian whiskey?" he asked quietly.

With a knowing sigh, Mrs. Crocker, heaved herself up. "Don't be telling your father I gave it to you is all. And don't drink so much that you can't do your duty by Princess Natilde, hear?"

"I want it so that I *can* do it." He sounded wry, a hint of a laugh behind it.

Fortunately neither he nor Mrs. Crocker appeared to notice Nix's reflexive start at the sound of her name. *Not anymore. Not ever again.* Nix studied her hands, fervently wishing to fade into the floor.

"Is she so terrible, then?" Mrs. Crocker sounded as if she gossiped with the royal family on a daily basis. "She looked lovely enough. Does her disposition not match her pretty face? Sorry, Nix, if you have an affection for your mistress and we offend you."

"I bear no affection for her, no," Nix whispered. She sensed the prince's eyes upon her again. Then his bootsteps sounded on the scrubbed stone floor, pausing next to her. His fingers on her chin, raising her face to meet his penetrating stare. He held the bottle of whiskey in his other hand and took a long drink as he studied her. "Your mistress would have had us send you out into the winter."

It sounded like a dare. A statement he clearly expected her to answer, though he didn't pose it as a question.

"I should go then," she managed, though her voice quavered at the prospect. Leave Falada? It would be the severest of blows, but not unexpected. But he did not release her. Instead those strangely hypnotic eyes held her fast, even as he took another swig of whiskey.

"Your people must be heartless, to accept such barbarity. I would no more abandon the infant heir I hope to get on your mistress to a blizzard than have you sent away in this season. You barely made it here in time. Winter is setting in firmly."

"Nix and I have been discussing what she might do." Mrs. Crocker had a soothing tone. Why should the prince need soothing and why would the housekeeper be the one to do it? "No one will be sent away."

"Good." The prince grunted the word, then took another pull of whiskey, still holding her chin, but gentling his grip, stroking the bones of her jaw, not unlike she'd settle Falada. "What have you hit upon?"

"We've yet to decide on the perfect place," Mrs. Crocker tempered with a diplomacy that surprised Nix. "She's not been here long and is still recovering from her journeys."

"Ah." The prince seemed to recall himself and released her. "Of course. I'll leave you to your duties and attend to my own." That wry tone again. He turned away, took a step, then spun back with such liquid grace she imagined he could have run her through before she knew it, had he a sword in his hand. "Your mistress—has she more of that perfume in her belongings?"

Impossible, given her nerves and despair, but Nix nearly laughed at the consternation on his face. Superstitious of bathing, the newly minted Princess Natilde had instead doused herself with the perfume she'd bought from a lady of Duranor they met at an inn, using Nix's coin. Nix would have warned her from using too much, even owing her only enmity, had the woman been inclined to listen at all. Suppressing the urge to smile at him, she shook her head. "I believe she used it…all. There is none left."

"This explains a great deal," he muttered, and drank of the whiskey yet again, gaze lingering on Nix.

"I'll take that liquor away from you, young buck," Mrs. Crocker scolded, "lest your whiskey dick leave you unable to perform."

Her face hot with scandalized shock, Nix goggled at the housekeeper, terrified that the prince would strike her down for her insolence. Instead he laughed, losing the brooding mien and sounding carefree, and suddenly much younger. Even more astonishing, he kissed the woman on the cheek and pinched her ample hip. "Aw, Brenna. Don't be jealous. You'll always be my first love."

Mrs. Crocker actually giggled, then made a swipe for the bottle, but he held it away from her, took one more long pull, then set it in front of Nix. "Here. What was it—Nix? You have the rest. You need some color and spirit. No more cringing like a ghost haunting our kitchens. You're not the one facing a burdensome fate, after all."

He'd gone back to mean and wry. Had he been forced into this marriage? Nix had thought him willing all along. At least as willing as she, with the hope they'd build something together. For the first time she considered her dire circumstances with a sense of reprieve. How would it have been to be the woman waiting upstairs as he sneered about her in the kitchen, fortifying himself for the dreaded duty of divesting her of her virginity? Perhaps he and Princess Natilde deserved each other.

The prince must have read some of it in her face because he shrugged and gave her a self-deprecating twist of his mouth. "Don't look so shocked, little ghost. With your mistress I shall be all that is gallant and noble. She'll never guess what's said of her in the kitchens. You'll keep my secrets, won't you?"

Unable to muster an answer, oddly flustered by his trust in her, she nodded. He ran a hand over her hair, then kissed her forehead with the same affection he'd shown Mrs. Crocker. Then, with a wink, slipped the whiskey from her hands and took one more drink before handing it back. "We who are about to fuck, salute you."

"Oh, go on with you now!" Mrs. Crocker plopped aggrieved fists on her hips, but laughter sparkled in her eyes.

The prince held up his hands as if surrendering and headed

to the doorway. Just before exiting, he turned back and pinned Nix with a discomfiting stare. "She likes horses," he said. "Something in the stables, perhaps."

~ 3 ~

PRINCE CAVAN LEFT as abruptly as he'd arrived, leaving Nix feeling rather as if she'd been battered by one of the squalls off the ocean. The room felt emptier for the absence of his ferocious and playful presence. How had he known she loved horses?

"I hope you don't mind his ways," Mrs. Crocker settled herself at the table again, taking the whiskey and pouring a generous helping in with the cooling tea in both of their mugs. "His Highness spent a great deal of time hanging about my skirts in these kitchens when he was young and still frequents from time to time. With the queen ill for so long, it was a refuge for him. I imagine things are not so informal where you come from."

Nix had no idea. She'd never set foot in her own castle kitchens and had never thought to. "I don't mind," she said.

"I love the prince as well as my own," Mrs. Crocker added, looking to the doorway as if Cavan still stood there. "Particularly with his mother passing so young. But also because he has a tender heart, more than he ought to have, for his station. He'd never say so, or go against the king and his duty, but this arranged marriage business goes hard on a man like him. Some men can marry without love, but I'm not sure my Cavan is one."

"Why did he agree then?" Nix asked tentatively, unsure if she wanted to hear the answer. Just as she'd never thought of the kitchens, it had never occurred to her that her husband might hate the thought of her.

"You imagine the nobles have more freedom than we, with all their riches and power." Mrs. Crocker nodded to herself, not needing Nix to confirm. "Those of us of lower stations may look upon them and envy their fine clothes. Perhaps you imagine if you were Princess Natilde, you could wave your hand and command yourself into a better situation."

Nix flinched, knowing just how untrue that was. How weak and pitiful she'd been. How easily brutalized and cowed.

It was only a week's ride from the small port on the coast to Castle Marcellum, the letters from King Wyn said. Queen Isyn, with her failing health and disaster on all fronts, had needed all her guard. Besides Erie held no danger. The messengers confirmed that. With High King Uorsin's famous peace, she and her waiting woman could travel on horseback through the rough hillside country far more quickly than with an armed guard and necessary supply caravan.

They hadn't counted on the cold, though. So much more wintery than the isles, and growing more uncomfortable with every league they traveled. Particularly when they found all the streams frozen, hours between inns and they had no water left in their bags.

Desperately thirsty, Nix had asked her waiting woman—a strange, dark-haired woman who'd volunteered to attend her in the foreign land—to break the ice and fill their canteens.

The woman, who'd been growing more abrasive by the day, sneered at her. "Get it yourself, *Princess.*"

She hadn't known how to handle that. A servant had never

refused her anything. So, she dismounted.

"I'll tie the horses," the serving woman offered, sounding meeker, so she'd agreed. Falada wouldn't wander off, but no one was to know her true identity. She wouldn't like it, but she'd put up with it to travel to this land where no one believed faeries existed, out of friendship for Nix.

Kneeling on the frozen mud of the bank, soiling her pretty gown, she took a rock and banged a hole in the ice. Not nearly as easy as it looked, but finally she broke through to water, a shock against her bare fingers.

"You'll want a bigger hole than that," the waiting woman advised, standing behind her. "You have to dip the canteen in, dummy."

Shocked, Nix sputtered. "You…you can't—"

"What, *Princess?* Mommy isn't here to help you now." The words, the ugly expression on the woman's face, chilled her more than the icy water. Moving slowly under the oppressive sense of looming terror, she worked to make the hole bigger, frantic flapping thoughts beating in her brain.

Hard hands hit her back, sending her sprawling onto the ice, half in the open hole she'd made. The water froze her lungs and stole her breath. She shook her head, trying to clear it. The white cambric with her mother's blood, the talisman, fell from her bodice and into the black water, swept away under the ice. With a cry, she reached for it, but those same rough hands seized her by the hair, yanking her back and dragging her up the bank. She clawed at the hands, but her fingers were numb, her brain still muzzy from knocking her head. Some ways away, Falada whinnied in anger.

"Here, *Princess.* Your clothes are all wet. Let me help you out of them." Rough fingers tore at her laces. The waiting woman had never been all that gentle with her assistance, but she lost all pretense of it, ripping at Nix's gown, scoring her skin with sharp nails. When Nix tried to push her off, the woman slapped her hard across the face, making her vision darken.

Nix gaped at the woman in shock, cradling her cheek.

"Never been struck in your whole pampered life, have you?" The woman slapped her again, then another time, red mouth curving in cruel pleasure. "You're just a weak, fearful child and you will kiss my feet when I'm done with you."

She stripped Nix of the gown, leaving her shivering in a thin silk sheath. "Let me just hang this up for you, *Princess*." More carefully than Nix expected, she did, taking it to a nearby tree and hanging the priceless gown from a branch and smoothing it to dry properly. Beyond her, Falada screamed in anger. She had been hard-tied to the tree so she couldn't break away. Both painful and humiliating.

"Falada!" Nix stood and took a step, the snow biting into her bare feet.

"Don't worry about her." The waiting woman returned with a length of rope. "You have lessons to learn. Put your back against that tree."

"I won't. Let me and Falada go and I won't report you."

"Oh, look at that spirit. I thought you had no spine at all." The woman grinned. Then punched Nix in the mouth, hard enough to draw blood. "But you are right that you won't report me. You'll never say anything about this to anyone. If you convince me, I might let you live."

She pushed Nix against the tree, easily out-muscling her, forcing her wrists to meet behind and tying them so tightly the coarse hemp dug in with brutal pain. The waiting woman dragged back Nix's ankles, too, looping the rope around one, then the other and shortening the rope so her thighs were spread.

The smile on the waiting woman's face when she came around to face Nix, made her cringe. "Please…"

"That's better." She stroked Nix's cheek. "But when you beg me, call me 'Princess Natilde'." Nix stared in shock and the woman slapped her, then stroked again. "What do you say?"

"Please, Princess Natilde," she whispered.

"Better!" The woman smiled cheerfully and nodded, petting her wet, snarled hair. "Now let's take a look at what King Wyn bought for his son." Pulling out a knife, she cut away the fragile underthings, ignoring Nix's pleas, deliberately scratching her with the point of the knife, laughing when Nix begged her to stop.

"Look at these pretty tits." The waiting woman squeezed them roughly. "Are you turned on, my little pet? Your paps are hard." She twisted Nix's tender nipples until she screamed. Let her sobbingly recover, then did it again.

"Please, Princess Natilde!" Nix moaned after what felt like hours. Her hands had gone numb from the ropes, her feet the same from the snow. She bled from various cuts and her nipples felt as if they might fall off. "I'll do anything. Give you anything. Please let me go."

"You do sound more humble." The woman tapped her chin thoughtfully. "Will you give me the Prince?"

Nix frowned, confused, then shrieked at the bite of the blade on her breast. "Yes! Yes, Princess Natilde. He's yours."

"And you'll never tell anyone."

"Never," Nix agreed over sobs.

"I'm going to make sure of it." The woman held up the dagger she'd been using to torment Nix, showing her the hilt.

"Meet your husband, little virgin."

She thrust the hilt between Nix's spread thighs, shoving it into her and rending her maidenhead. It might as well have been the blade end, the way it hurt. But Nix had lost what little fight she'd possessed. She only wept as the hilt raped her.

"Do you like this?" The woman pumped this in and out of her. "It's much better than your prince would have done. Thank me for it and I'll stop."

"Thank you, Princess Natilde," she cried, unbearably grateful to have the invasion removed.

"Good pet." She held up the bloodied hilt. "Your virgin blood. You're worthless now. The *one* thing that made you valuable is gone. Poof! Like magic. Shall I leave you here? Now that you're ruined, I'm sure any passersby would be happy to help themselves, even if you aren't so pretty anymore." She made a little moue of her mouth. "You might freeze first, though, and I did promise to let you go. If I do, will you be a good little pet?

"Yes, Princess Natilde." Anything to stop the torment.

"I'm going to untie you. You will get on your knees and kiss my feet. If you convince me you're sincere, I'll generously give you my dress and you'll help me into yours. Understand? You get one chance to do this right."

Of course she agreed. When the ropes loosened, she fell to the snow naked, her feet unable to hold her weight, drops of blood marring the white. She kissed Princess Natilde's feet, over and over, swearing to silence, shivering so hard she could barely speak.

Finally the princess stroked her hair, then lifted her chin. "You've done well, so I'm willing to let you live. Here are the rules. I am Princess Natilde and you will never say otherwise to anyone. I know that monster you call a horse can talk. If it says otherwise, ever, I will have it killed and its head hung where you will have to see it, every day. The next three nights are a test. If you're good at the inns, stay silent and serve me well, I'll let you go free once we reach Castle Marcellum. Agreed?"

"Yes, Princess Natilde."

"I'm doing you a favor you know. Prince Cavan would have found you most disappointing. But keep this in mind—if you forget and think to tell him who you were, he'll find out you're no longer a virgin. He'll cut your throat. King Wyn will be outraged. Maybe he'll send armies to your precious Isles. Think of all that, pet. Now, beg me for these clothes."

Nix hadn't stopped thinking about it, much as she wished she could. The bruises and cuts throbbed still, though days old, and she felt as if she'd never be warm again. But the dark shame pained her far more.

Her soul might never recover.

She started when Mrs. Crocker touched her hand, then tapped a purple-scabbed bruise on Nix's wrist, where the ropes had cut in. "A servant's life can be hard, but so can a prince's. He might not suffer beatings from his betters, it's true. All of us, though, king or pauper, do what we must. Prince Cavan has a responsibility to the throne and his people. The alliance with your kingdom will improve many lives and he knows it. It's worth it to him, to sacrifice a bit of personal happiness for that end. You understand?"

Nix understood why Cavan liked to visit Mrs. Crocker in her kitchen, if nothing else.

"No one here will beat you, child," the housekeeper said kindly. "Nor will you be sent away. You heard the prince. This is your chance to find your own bit of happiness. What responsibilities would you like best?"

The whiskey burned through the tea, warming her throat and the chill ball of terror that had lodged all these days in her belly, as if thrust there by her serving woman's rough fingers, by the violation of that rough-carved hilt. "The stables," she whispered. How Cavan had known, she had no idea, but there she'd be with Falada. And away from Princess Natilde's sight.

Mrs. Crocker frowned a little. "There's not much for you there. We have the stable lads, the grooms." She snapped her fingers. "I know. The geese. You can mind them. There's a young man, Conrad—a bit younger than you are—that does it, but the geese can be worse than herding kittens and he can always use another pair of hands and eyes."

Geese. She could mind geese. Something simple.

"You'll sleep near them in the stables, to be sure they don't set up a fuss—which they do if disturbed, or out of just plain ornery nature. In the mornings, you take them out to graze and swim a bit, then round them up come sundown. Easy enough?"

"Yes, ma'am." It sounded all right.

"It will get you out in the sun a bit. Cavan is right—you're a pale wisp of a thing. We'll get you set to rights. You'll see. All will work out fine in the end."

THE SERVING GIRL'S haunted eyes, a bruised blue in her shivering white face, stayed with Cavan as he paced his chambers, waiting for notice that his bride had finished her bath and awaited him. He wished fervently he'd brought the whiskey up with him. Brenna had a point about the danger of whiskey dick, particularly on top of his keenly felt physical reservations, but that hadn't been why he left the bottle behind. He'd felt strangely moved to give the girl something. To soothe the trembling that took her when he touched her chin, to calm the skittish terror in her eyes.

Servants were beaten all the time, though not in Marcellum, or even most of Erie, the same courtesy they afforded the horses and other livestock. He could hardly fault his new bride, however, for following an otherwise common practice. Or he wouldn't, if he liked her better than he did. He needed to shake this instant aversion he'd developed for Natilde and give her time to demonstrate her good qualities. Judging her harshly would get them nowhere. It might not even have been her mistress who'd visited the scrapes and bruises on tiny Nix.

An ill-fated name, indeed. He'd given her the whiskey partly out of fear she'd fade to nothing at all. Though the fate of this foreign servant girl shouldn't matter.

She shouldn't have captured any of his attention, truly. Far too timid—almost irritatingly so—fragile as a sunbeam on new snow, her hair so blond it resembled the ivory of his favorite chess set. Unreasonable that she pulled at him, that he'd even for a moment considered cuddling her close, caressing that petal-thin skin and stroking her until she shivered with delight instead of the quavering of an abused hound dog. Until she welcomed him into her slight body, her slender hands like flowers on his skin, his name sighing on her breath like a warm breeze.

Impossible that he entertained such thoughts at all, let alone on his wedding night. To another woman.

Yet those fantasies of her worked to rouse him in a way that all his previous determined imaginings had not. His cock, steadfastly uninterested in duty or responsibility up to this point, stirred and hardened. Going to the window, Cavan looked down at the now empty inner yard, violet with dusk, and pictured Nix again as she'd been, leaning against the horse, murmuring to it, delicate white hands moving over the mare in a kind of benediction. Almost he could believe in enchantments, the way the horse had gazed at her with rapt affection, and seemed to speak to her in turn.

Nonsense, but he stroked himself over his clothes, preserving the arousal, fantasizing that he might sweep her up onto his horse, pull her to straddle him and ride him in turn. With her fey build, she'd be light enough, barely a feather as she clung to him, her ivory hair spilling around them, her slight breasts pink and white as the cherry blossoms of spring. He slowed, needing now to hold back what his body urged, saving the arousal to service his bride.

Good timing, too, as his valet knocked just then and informed him Princess Natilde invited him to join her. Holding firmly to his warm thoughts—after all, it mattered not whose visage he held in his head and it did matter that he manage to perform—he strode down the hall and entered the bridal chambers for a second time.

Natilde had changed into a peignoir, gossamer thin and nearly transparent. It seemed too small for her, though he supposed such garments were made to be. Her full breasts strained the silk, dark nipples thrust as boldly as her sensual gaze, the dark thatch at her thighs as lush as the rippling chestnut waves flowing down her back. Would little Nix have ivory hair at her sex, like a lace of frost barely veiling the pink that would peek through? Guilt at the disloyal thought pricked him, but it also rejuvenated the lust that had flagged at the sight of his bride and the chill at the triumphant tilt of her smile.

Taking Natilde's hand, he brushed it with a kiss, relieved to find the heavy perfume mostly gone. Nix had nearly laughed at his question, the somber blue lighting with a glint quickly banished. The princess would not have listened to advice on heavy scent, but Nix had known. Perhaps had even mischievously kept silent. It made him smile to think of it—and tempted him to see what it would take to coax more mischief from her guarded self.

"What makes you smile, husband?" Natilde asked, eyes narrowing as if she could read his thoughts indeed.

"Pleasure how beautiful you look," he returned smoothly. His wife would not catch him out in the lie. He'd trained too well for too long to present only what the world should see. Determined to see the consummation through immediately, lest his enthusiasm flag again, he led her to the bed and helped her onto it, then eased her into lying back. She pulled him with her, a sensation uncomfortably like being sucked underwater by a tangle of old submerged limbs. His instincts shouted at him to kick away from the danger, but he firmly directed his thoughts back to the fantasy of Nix's gleaming arms, her hair spread beneath them, white as bone.

Natilde's mouth parted under his, hot and provocative. His bride. His queen. Mother of his heirs and bringer of prosperity to the lands. His destiny and accepted fate. Even as he pushed up her gown and her eager hands freed his cock, the bleakness of the future rolled out in his mind's eye, a winter that never ended. She stroked him deftly, coaxing his flagging member back to full attention. Not her hands, but the image of Nix doing the same did the trick, touching him as she'd touched her mare. Natilde moved urgently under him, guiding him to her entrance. Nix's waifish blue eyes seemed to accuse him, so he tore his mouth from Natilde's and pressed his lips to her collarbone, imaging it as the delicate wing he'd glimpsed above Nix's rough garment. Her silken skin under his tongue.

With Nix firmly fixed in his mind, he thrust into his bride's body. She cried out in delight, a sound not unlike a warrior beheading his enemy on the battlefield, and wound her thighs around his hips. He pumped into her willing body, on the downhill crash now, ready to release his seed to her fertile soil, thinking now of the sons and daughters they would make. They would be his joy, his family.

Complete the alliance, get an heir, then dally with all the maids you like.

It no longer sounded vile, but like a promise. His reward for completing his duty to the throne. Once he got Natilde with child, she would be content to breed and he would seek out Nix. Perhaps by the time spring arrived, he'd hold her sweet body in his arms, have her kisses rain upon him with the benediction of her gentle spirit.

With a cry, a surge of triumphant relief, he spilled his seed into his bride. He'd managed it. Done as he should. Natilde cried out her own pleasure, fortunately, as he hadn't had the wit or, to be honest, the interest in seeing to it. It made him a terrible person. Even as he collapsed upon her, buried in her slick flesh, sweat soaking their garments, he felt no affection for her. If anything, he forced away a sense of growing revulsion, of terrible wrong.

"Husband," Natilde murmured in a tone of deepest pleasure.

It took everything he had not to deny it.

~ 4 ~

THE STABLES TURNED out to be very fine, indeed. Far more so than Nix had imagined they might be. Of course, she'd no more stepped foot into the stables at home than she had the kitchens. Falada, as befit her elevated status, as resident Court Faery and companion to the princess, had enjoyed her own small cottage, designed to suit her specifications and with a door she could operate herself, to either go out and enjoy a run or close against chilly weather.

The geese were kept in a room off the main stables and Mrs. Crocker led her there by a path that did not take them past the stalls. Nix would have to find Falada later. When Mrs. Crocker opened the door, the geese set up a racket, their honking quickly hitting a bass crescendo that had Nix clapping her hands over her ears.

"Hey now!" A young lad—probably several years younger than she—came around the corner, face red with irritation. "Who in the Twelve—oh, Mrs. Crocker."

"Conrad." She gave him a placid look that nevertheless conveyed a warning. She closed the door on the geese. "You're not in with the geese?"

He looked abashed. "I was just on my way back. You'll see they were already settled."

"Well, I have help for you, so you can take turns staying with the fretful creatures. This is Nix, our new goose girl."

Far from seeming pleased, Conrad wrinkled his nose at her. "I handle the geese."

"Now you'll have four hands. Once Nix learns the tricks of the trade, perhaps we can move you up to stable lad or even groom."

That appeased him. He lost his black scowl and looked Nix over. "Fine. I'll teach you what you need to know."

"Thank you." It wasn't difficult to sound meek. Her old self might have laughed at the boy, for pompously sounding like herding geese took great skill. But her old self hadn't realized how little she really knew how to do. Or how little worth she possessed.

Mrs. Crocker noticed her shiver. "I'll get you some warm clothes and bedding. You'll be just fine." She patted Nix's shoulder, reminding her of the kiss Cavan had planted on her forehead. These people touched far more than hers did.

Once she'd gone, Conrad drew himself up in grave self-importance. "The first rule is to keep the geese calm and quiet. If they get riled up, they'll keep half the castle up all night and you don't want to see what happens then!"

She nodded, following him around the corner to a small room with a bed and an unlit lamp. A half wall overlooked the goose pen, their continuing indignant honks echoing off the walls as they strutted about, hissing and flapping wings.

"Since you riled 'em up, you can settle 'em down. Consider it your first test." Conrad awarded Nix another of his superior smiles, then abandoned the field, back to whatever he'd been doing when Mrs. Crocker caught him out.

Nix didn't mind. Being left alone now felt comforting and

allowed her the time she needed to settle her stomach after the wrench at being reminded of tests. She had a little room with a door to bar and something to do. Something, surprisingly enough, that she might know how to do—though it would never have occurred to her to articulate it to Mrs. Crocker. Settling herself on the low wall, she dangled her feet over and began to sing a song of her mother's, a very simple magic. The ancient strains came to her easily, the words in a language long since lost. But she shaped them carefully, knowing the curve and glide of them by heart. There wasn't much magic in the Twelve, but the song didn't require much. It soothed her to sing it, though the soft sounds didn't rise above the chaos at first. Gradually, though, the geese quieted, turning bright black eyes to her and folding their wings.

She sang them back into sleep, into a slumber so peaceful that not one fluttered a feather when Mrs. Crocker knocked, bringing a wooden box with her when Nix opened the door to the little room. She cocked her head at the peaceful sight and raised her brows. "Sing to them where you come from, do you? Never thought of such a thing. Works a charm though. Pretty song, too. Didn't know you spoke a different language there."

"We don't," Nix offered, feeling a little shy to be discovered. "It's an old song, an ancient dialect, from before Common Tongue."

"Ah," Mrs. Crocker nodded, though she clearly didn't understand. Perhaps, along with no magic, they also lacked old songs. "I brought you blankets, some warm clothes for tomorrow, supper for tonight and more tea. Here's a stand with a candle, to keep the pot warm. You're welcome to come eat in the kitchen with the other servants, but something made me think you'd rather be alone tonight."

She did, taking the things with relieved gratitude.

"Good. I snuck you a bit of what the prince and princess will be having. After all, I figure, it's your first night here, too." Then Mrs. Crocker cleared her throat and fished out a squat glass jar with a cork in the wide mouth. "This is a balm I brew, for bruises and such. Use it well, child."

Unexpectedly, Nix's eyes filled with tears. It shouldn't have reminded her, with the setting, the circumstances so different, but the memory rushed back of her mother, a few forever-ago weeks before. The queen's long illness had sapped much of her strength, but she'd called Nix to her chambers and bade her hold vigil while she worked the enchantment. With a sharp knife, she cut her own finger, letting three drops of blood fall onto a piece of white cambric. Giving the cloth to Nix, she'd said, "I regret I cannot go with you, but I give you this, my heart's blood. Keep it with you always and know you have my protection. Use it well, child."

But she'd lost it under the ice, in that same irrevocable way she'd lost herself. Mortified, Nix wiped away the tears and Mrs. Crocker frowned at her.

"Is there aught you need to tell me, little Nix?"

"No." Nix shook her head vigorously. "I'm just tired and grateful to you, for everything."

"All right then." Mrs. Crocker glanced over the slumbering geese. "I expect we're grateful to have you, too."

After Mrs. Crocker departed, Nix ate the delicious meal, then slipped out to find Falada. They'd given her a roomy box stall, at least, but Falada gazed at her balefully.

"I feel like a prisoner," she said, when Nix let herself in.

"I'm so sorry. I'll set you loose and you can run free. Or make your way home."

"No, Princess. Your mother sent me with you and I'll stay. I'll see this through." Falada lipped her hair and Nix leaned into the horse's warm strength.

"Don't call me that anymore," she whispered. "I can't bear to hear it—and I told them my name is Nix."

"If your mother only knew, her heart would break."

"She can't ever know."

"It's my fault she has power over you still," Falada said in a sorrowful tone. "It's mete that I should suffer also."

"I'm the one who let it happen, who didn't fight hard enough."

Somehow that failure galled her as much as anything.

CUSTOM DICTATED THAT Cavan stay closeted with his bride, so they dined together in the bridal chambers. When he'd planned the meal with Brenna, he'd indulged in a fit of idealism, thinking perhaps he and Natilde would eat it together in bed, feeding each other morsels, so he'd chosen finger foods with tasty sauces. Abysmal decision, in retrospect. The supper only made the lack of romantic intimacy between him and his new bride more starkly apparent.

For her part, she fell on the food with gusto—and unfortunate manners. He dispatched his share quickly, all the while calculating how long until he could gracefully withdraw. Not for hours yet, certainly, as the castle denizens expected him to service the new princess numerous times. Fortunately custom also decreed that they keep separate sleeping chambers going forward.

Natilde had changed into an ivory velvet robe, which also

seemed to be too small, her generous breasts straining against the low neckline. Catching his look and mistaking it for one of interest, Natilde smiled at him across the narrow table, and licked sauce from her fingers. It should have been appealing, but was somehow… animal. Falling woefully short of the sensual scene he'd so foolishly imagined.

"Ready for another round of rutting, husband?"

He caught himself before he frowned at her for the crude question, but she seemed to catch his discomfort, raising her brows in mockery. Nix had blushed, delicate pink infusing the winter white of her cheeks, when he and Brenna teased each other in the kitchen, as if truly scandalized. She couldn't be an innocent, no matter how young she looked. Servants lived earthier lives and learned rough language early. But a servant girl wasn't a princess, no matter how dainty she appeared. Had Brenna found a place for her? He squelched the impulse to go find out. He'd abandoned his bride once. Twice would begin to look suspicious.

"I merely noticed that your robe seems small. Is it comforta-ble?"

Natilde laughed and clasped her breasts, lifting them lewdly. "These things just spill out of everything! But you bring up a good point. I need new clothes, lots of them."

"I'll ask the seamstresses to attend you tomorrow."

"Good. And I need the jewels that were sent ahead."

Now Cavan did frown. "They were part of your dowry and I believe King Wyn had everything catalogued and added to the royal treasury."

Natilde's eyes narrowed, going poison green in her displeas-ure. "They're *mine*."

Had his princess been raised with no sense of responsibility or duty to their combined people? "Natilde," he said carefully, feeling his way through the diplomatic bog he hadn't expected from his wife, "you understand the terms of the alliance, yes?"

"Of course!" She drank her wine and poured more. "I'm not an idiot, you know."

"The thought never crossed my mind. So you understand that the dowry—everything your mother sent—is earmarked to fund what we need to do to consolidate our two kingdoms." And to pay High King Uorsin's extortionate tithe to allow the merging, even though it added to his realm.

"It can't be that expensive," she replied airily, waving a hand. "Keep the gold cups and silver trinkets. I just want my jewels."

"It *will* be expensive. Your people have suffered great privations from the flood-ruined crops and resulting plagues. We will have to move armies to shore up your defenses against Koonce-lund's aggression. Possibly even hire mercenaries. We have the experience and ability to do what needs to be done, but your dowry will be funding it. We need every piece and then some. I thought you knew all of this."

Her mouth took a mean slant. "You just don't want me to be happy. And here it is, my wedding night. Has any bridegroom been more cruel?"

Cavan fought down his impatience, his burgeoning distaste. Instead of growing fonder in her company, he only seemed to dislike her more. At that moment, he'd have traded her "pleasant visage" for the character of a true queen, who would do true credit to the throne. How could this have gone so dramatically wrong? And now they were stuck together, the marriage and alliance sealed. It made him ill to contemplate an endless future of this.

"Cat got your tongue?" Natilde jibed, wetting her lush lips.

"I hope not because I plan to have you use it on me."

"Forgive me," he said abruptly and stood. What in the name of Danu was he doing? "I'm afraid something in the food has unsettled my gut. Please excuse me."

With that weak excuse, and before she could muster past her shock to reply, he strode out of the room. The servants in the anteroom gaped at him with the same astonishment, their expressions so a reflection of Natilde's that he wondered how he looked. Unable to find it in himself to smooth his expression, he offered them the same explanation, then bolted for his own rooms, sending away his valet and barring the door, as if truly ill, indeed.

~ 5 ~

T HE NEXT MORNING, gossip everywhere had it that Prince Cavan had taken ill and had been forced to retire alone. Nix had always known the servants talked and news spread among them like fire in late summer grass, but this was her first time to be part of it. It nearly shocked her, how much everyone knew of the supposedly intimate events in the bridal chamber. The marriage had been consummated, so word was that no insult had been given to Princess Natilde, the king and queen were pleased to have the alliance sealed and Cavan's illness was expected to be minor and quickly gone.

The prince's sudden indisposition had prevented more than one bedding and Natilde had been vocal in her unhappiness to her new maids. Several sly whispers hinted that Cavan had looked more angry than ill and many speculated he did not care for his new bride.

Nix thought of the laughing, wry man who'd chugged whiskey in the kitchen while teasing her, how he'd touched her with concern, and hoped it hadn't been overindulging that made him sick. More, she worried that Natilde had done something to him, in her sly cruelty. Perhaps she'd found a way to hurt and deceive him, also. He was a man, much bigger and stronger than Nix, but Natilde loomed large in her mind, radiating menace. It pained her stomach to remember what had happened by the stream, how the woman had raped her with the dagger hilt while she described how the prince would fuck her instead, licking Nix's tears and making her say how much she liked it.

But she hadn't. It had made her ill and, though it made no sense, she worried something of the same had happened to Cavan.

She had no choice, though, but to keep her head down and concentrate on the task she'd been given. Conrad, no less supercilious than the night before, but pleased that the geese had caused no trouble, showed her how to open the outer doors for the birds to trot happily out. Though the sun hadn't quite broken the horizon, despite the late hour, the sky had cleared and held the promise of blue when it lightened fully. The sun set earlier here and rose later than at home. Another reminder of her changed circumstances, as if she could forget. But a night of sleep with her pains eased by Mrs. Crocker's balm and without the fear of further torture put Nix in a better, if not exactly peaceful, then less terrorized frame of mind. Despite the crisp cold of the air, it felt good to be walking with Conrad, following the geese on their familiar path, out the side gate, through an archway in the outer walls, and past the village.

The road streamed with activity that the geese serenely ignored, self-importantly waddling along on the verge, certain of their direction. Wagons laden with food and other supplies passed them going the other direction, carrying their burdens to the castle or the village market. As promised, Erie enjoyed far greater prosperity than her ravaged isles, even with the winter so bitter. If Cavan made as good a king as his father did, her people would be far better off for this alliance that would rescue them from the long decline caused by natural disasters, an aggressive neighbor and an ailing ruler. A warming thought in the waste-land of her heart.

The geese turned off at a path and followed it down through a snow-covered pasture to a pond frozen at the edges, with open water at the center. They took to the water with enthusiasm, flapping their clipped wings and seeming not to care that they skidded across ice to get to it, paddling around and diving under without a flinch for the freezing temperatures. Nix shivered for them, remembering the chill of the stream and her sodden dress, soaking her to the bone. Despite the layers of clothes she'd donned, that ice never seemed to leave her blood.

Conrad patrolled the perimeter of the lake, reminding her of the geese with his puffed-up strutting. He carried a staff—to fight off any wolves that might attack he told her—and spent a great deal of time staring suspiciously into the woods, then looking to see if Nix had noticed. What she mainly discovered was that the winter day, even with the bright sunlight, made it far too cold to sit. She began pacing a circle around the lake also, keeping an eye on the geese, following the path worn in by many feet.

"I'm watching for wolves." Conrad strode up to her on her circuit. "That's a man's job. You are to watch the geese."

"I am watching the geese," she returned mildly, "and trying not to freeze to death."

"Cold, are you?"

"A little."

Conrad's expression shifted into something unsettling. Much as she'd seen on her serving woman's face, just before…

"You have such pretty hair," Conrad reached to grab a lock, but she jumped back in time. Not again. Never again.

"Where are you going?" he chased after as she backed up,

unsteady on the frozen mud. "I just want to touch your pretty hair."

"No. Desist immediately." In her fear, the curling sense of nausea, she forgot and shut him down with all the regal poise she'd learned over the years and that had eluded her in her shock and consternation over losing the talisman. Confused by it, and well-accustomed to obeying that tone, Conrad halted. Then glared at her.

"You're not special—you rank lower than me."

"I'm a goose girl, not your doxy."

"Fine." He thrust the staff at her. "You can fend off the wolves. Or get eaten. See if I care."

He left her there in his righteous fury, probably hoping she'd call after him. But apparently something remained of her shredded pride because she managed not to. The sudden truth of it took her by surprise, that she'd rather face wolves and the possibility of being their prey than the prospect of anyone putting their hands on her like that again.

A good thing to know about herself, that she had some resolve still. She might be a goose girl, but she could make a life of that. She might be trapped as surely as the geese, her wings clipped and her life as circumscribed. But the world held far more horrifying fates.

She'd survived and that was something to cling to.

CAVAN MET WITH his father privately in the morning, ostensibly to report on the Princess Natilde, but truthfully in the hopes that his father might give him much-needed perspective. And advice on dealing with his distaste for her. King Wyn listened without interrupting—as was his habit and discipline, to hear out any tale or petition to the end before he formed an opinion—then stroked his beard when Cavan finished, thinking.

"Princess Natilde is quite young," he finally said. "She is far from home, newly married, bedded to a stranger and divested of her innocence. It would be surprising if she had not acted emotionally, no matter how gently you treated her. Give her what she asks for, so she can feel secure in her new home. If having jewels makes her happy, let her have them. You have many years to learn each other. The more she feels cherished by you, the easier she will be to work with in the future."

Cavan doubted that, having glimpsed the shallowness of her heart, but he did not argue. His father's words pricked at his guilt, that he had not treated Natilde gently. In truth, she'd been so expert at handling him that he'd forgotten her virginity. Still, it hadn't seemed to hurt her and she'd prodded him for more. Which he would have to muster the will to do.

"Remember that she is a foreigner in her ways. We may speak the same language, but that does not mean we naturally communicate well. Be patient and learn to look past the difference in manners."

"You're right, of course. I just need to get to know her better."

"Get her with child," the king advised. "Women settle when they have babes to grow and care for. And she no doubt feels the responsibility to get an heir as much as you do. She'll forget trifles such as jewels when she discovers the pricelessness of a child." He clasped Cavan's shoulder. "I did. You are my greatest treasure, my son. I'm proud of you for how you've handled this."

Moved, Cavan searched for words. "It's the right thing, this alliance. I'll find a way to make this marriage work."

With renewed resolve—and chagrined to have lost sight of the bigger picture—Cavan arranged to have the seamstresses sent to his bride, with instructions to make her as many gowns as she wished for. He visited the treasury and asked to see Natilde's dowry, something he hadn't given much thought to, beyond converting it into currency to aid her people and his own. It was an impressive array of riches, indeed, and he filled a chest with all the jewelry he could find, intent on carrying it to her himself.

He stopped by the kitchens on his way. Partly out of long habit and more than a little with the sense of reaching for his touchstone. Consult with his father and confess to the woman who'd been a mother to him. Brenna spotted him and, with a long look, pointed him to sit at the table. She scooted several of the kitchen girls along on various duties, emptying the room, pulled some warm cookies out of the oven and set them before him. Still raw from the talk with his father, Cavan took a cookie with a profound sense of gratitude and tasted in it all the love Brenna had showered on him from his earliest childhood.

He needed to stop behaving like a spoiled brat and show Natilde the same care.

"Sick, were you?" Brenna raised an eyebrow. "I should not have let you have at that whiskey."

"It wasn't the whiskey," he replied, shamed to admit it to her, but holding his own feet to the fire. "I just needed to… get over myself, I guess."

Brenna nodded and took a cookie. "You'll do, my boy. It's not easy, acquiring a wife, one who is a stranger to you and with foreign ways to boot. You'll find your way."

Her faith and understanding took him another step toward

seeing it possible. "How is little Nix?" he asked. A reasonable question, given their encounter the night before. It betrayed nothing of how she'd gotten under his skin. A good ruler should take interest in even the least of his subjects.

Brenna sighed. "She's a wounded thing. I'm a bit concerned for her."

"How do you mean?" *Wounded.* Yes, he'd noted the same look in her eyes.

"It's hard for young serving women. They're easily abused by the world. Your thought was a good one though, and I've given her a chamber in the stables, with a door she can lock, and tasked her to watch the geese."

"The geese?"

"An easy job to start, one that gets her out of the castle and gives her time with her thoughts. Young Conrad goes with her still, in case they meet with wolves."

"Good." He supposed that should be enough, to know her settled. That should let him concentrate his own jumbled thoughts on Natilde. *No more fantasies of Nix.* He stood and picked up the chest of jewelry. "I'd best go see my bride. Thank you for the cookies."

"Take some to the princess, if you like."

An excellent idea. The more peace offerings, the better. A simple way to share the taste of love he couldn't find in himself.

He found her surrounded by a dozen seamstresses, her chambers piled high with fabrics of every imaginable color and texture. And in a fine sulk.

"Well look what the cat dragged in," she snapped at him. "Done puking and shitting?"

Several of the seamstresses blanched and one gasped. *Be patient and learn to look past the difference in manners.* He could learn to forgive what seemed crude to him and show her by example.

"Yes, my lady wife," he gave her a courtly bow. "I am much improved today. I apologize for my churlishness last night—and I've brought you gifts to make up for it." He presented her with the plate of warm cookies. "My favorite childhood treat. A sweet way to start your morning."

With a growl, she dashed the plate from his hand. It hit a seamstress on the cheek and the cookies went flying. Glaring at him, Natilde stepped off the stool she'd stood on and deliberately placed her bare foot on one of the cookies, grinding it into the priceless rug. "*That* is what I think of your pitiful apology! You disgust me. If you want to appease me, give me what I asked for."

Demanded, he wanted to correct her, but choked down his hurt and fury. Ridiculous to be wounded by the sight of the cookie crushed under her uncaring foot. *Her ways are not ours*, he reminded himself, and presented her with the casket of jewelry. "Will this suit better?"

She seized the heavy chest, set it on a table and flung open the lid with a squeal. Laughing, she pulled out the precious gems and began draping herself with them. Cavan tried his best to enjoy her pleasure, to appreciate that she seemed to be happy with this. His father had a point. He still had much to learn about governing himself.

Natilde turned a glowing look on him and sauntered close, winding her arms around his neck and rubbing her lush bosom against him. "This suits *much* better," she crooned. "See? We can learn to get along with each other."

"Indeed." He kept himself from pulling away. "Enjoy your fitting. Is there aught else you need?"

"Probably, but I'll send for it if I do. Unless you mean for me to pass all requests through you?"

A sharp prick of insult there, but one he likely deserved. "Not at all, Princess. This is your home now. Your word is anyone's command, as much as mine."

That pleased her and she wriggled against him. "And you'll attend me this evening? We have an heir to beget."

"I look forward to it." On pretext of giving her a courtly bow, he escaped her grasp and left the room, acutely aware of the enormity of his lie.

~ 6 ~

CONRAD NEVER DID return, but the geese knew their routine. As the sun descended in its early decline, the afternoon dimming into grays, the geese began to gather around her, expectant. She counted them all as present and started up the path, the birds forming an escort around her as dignified as any of her ladies had back home. It made her smile to think of it, how offended those ladies would be by the comparison—and her current circumstances. If just one of them had been brave enough to leave home, none of this would have happened.

If your mother only knew, her heart would break.

But it had been one of the nicer days she'd spent in a long while. Especially once Conrad took himself off and she found her pattern of walking. Watching the geese was peaceful, something her life hadn't been since the betrothal and the whirlwind of preparations to leave home. On the road to the castle, she passed a few of the same farmers and merchants as she had that morning and they nodded to her in greeting.

Back at the stables, the geese eagerly poured into their warm pen. Then set up a fuss, honking at her. She tried singing to them, but they only surged and teemed, hissing and snapping at her skirts.

"I believe they want their grain."

Nix whirled, startled to see Prince Cavan looking in the open half-door from the yard, his horse's reins in one hand, as the handsome stallion also peered in with bright interest.

"Forgive me, Your Highness." She hastily curtseyed, remembering herself, casting her eyes down in respect. "I didn't know you were there."

"Nothing to forgive—who could hear a thing over that ruckus?"

Her face heated. "I know I'm supposed to keep them quiet, but I'm still new at this. Grain then? I'll find it."

The prince nodded at a stable lad who hastened up to take the stallion's reins. "Fetch a bucket of whatever grain the geese get, would you?"

The boy nodded and led the horse off. As if they knew their supper would be on the way, the geese settled, still pacing expectantly, but thankfully without the honking and hissing.

Nix curtseyed again, not sure what else to do. "Thank you, Your Highness. I am abashed that you had to arrange that for me. I promise to do better in the future."

"No worries." He leaned against the doorframe and folded his arms in a relaxed pose, showing no sign of moving on. "Wasn't young Conrad to show you the ropes?"

How did he know that? The prince smiled at her, that bright, easy flash of a grin he'd given Mrs. Crocker. "You look so shocked. I asked Brenna what place had been found for you. Is that so surprising?"

"No, Your Highness…I mean, ah—" She cut herself off, thoroughly flustered and annoyed with herself for it. Then she met his gaze as he waited for her to finish, amusement lightening the gray of his eyes to sparkling silver. "Yes. It is surprising to me. I—it would not have happened back home."

He shrugged a little, eyes wandering over the goose pen, then back to her. "My father believes a good ruler should know all the workings of his kingdom. God is in the details, he says."

"It shows. Everything here runs so smoothly. It's good to see how much Remus will benefit from this alliance. We have much to learn from you."

Tilting his head quizzically, the prince opened his mouth to say something, but stopped as the stable lad raced up with a bucket of grain. "Prince Cavan," he panted and bowed.

"Thanks, Jeb." The prince let himself in and gave her that easy smile. "Let's see if I still have my skills."

"You've fed geese before?" She found herself smiling back, as warmed as if the summer sun shone on her.

"I was a curious boy and made a nuisance of myself." He scattered the grain evenly, flicking it to the far corners to distract the geese that shoved in to crowd the center. "The advantage of being a prince is no one tells you to go away, much as they might have wanted to."

"Queen Isyn wouldn't let…Princess Natilde wander like that. Certainly not with the servants. The court there is much more formal."

He looked thoughtful, scattering another handful of grain. "Is she a remote ruler then, perhaps cruel to Natilde?"

"Oh no! Never think that." Nix forgot herself in her haste to defend her mother. "My—Queen Isyn is, was, protective of Natilde. She lost many babies and children over the years and Natilde was the only to survive to adulthood."

"Spoiled her then?"

"I never heard anyone say so," Nix answered honestly, hoping that it was true. She'd never felt spoiled because she'd always been keenly aware of her responsibilities. Still… "Pampered, perhaps. Maybe coddled more than she should have been." If she'd been less soft, she might have found a way to stop what had happened.

Cavan nodded. "Thank you. That's helpful to know. My gratitude." He handed her the half-full grain bucket, his eyes somber, even sad, and she realized he'd been interested to know for his dealings with his bride. She'd forgotten, in the easiness of their conversation, that aspect. More, her worry prompted her to ask after his wellbeing. Which, of course, she could not.

He was a good man. Thoughtful and full of integrity, along with his playful nature and earnest interest in all life offered. He would have made her a fine husband and she, in her many failings, had stuck him with a terrible wife.

"I'm happy to be of service," she told him, meaning much more, wanting to offer comfort. To stroke the black fall of hair back from his forehead and kiss his brow as he had hers, this handsome prince she'd been meant to wed, had she not been so weak. Or, rather, who she had wed, all but for the final con-summation. With a horrified shock, it hit her that this man *was*, in fact, her husband. She could never wed another without violating her vows. And he, unknowingly, had violated his own by lying with the woman he thought was Natilde. She'd caused this noble and honest man to forswear himself, all through her cowardice and terror.

All she could do now was ensure he'd never know it. She could spare him that much.

NIX HAD LOST color, going whiter than a ghost, and swaying slightly as her mouth formed a horrified O. Cavan nearly looked behind him, to set what upset her, but her deep blue gaze remained fixed on him.

"What's wrong?" He took the bucket from her and tossed out the remaining grain, uncaring now if the geese fought over it. Her delicate hands felt like ice in his and she swallowed back some reply, ducking her eyes and then tugging away, though he held tight.

"Forgive me, Your Highness," she gasped. "I forgot myself."

"Don't give me that. Your manners are impeccable." Exquisite, even—a thought that gave him pause. "Something upset you." He reviewed the conversation in his mind. What had set her off? *I'm happy to be of service*, she'd said, and it hit him, along with Brenna's words. *It's hard for young serving women. They're easily abused by the world.* "Nix." He spoke gently, folding her hands in his to warm them. "Never think that I'd ask you to, ah, service me… in that way."

Her eyes, a startled blue flew to his, her pink lips parted, ivory hair taking on a golden hue in the lamplight. The desperate urge to kiss her, to devour that sweet mouth, to take down her hair so he could run his hands through it, put the lie to his words. Something she clearly read in his face, a rose flush easing over her pale cheeks. Needing to prove his restraint, both to her and to himself, he let go of her hands and stepped back.

"You're safe here, Nix. Even from me." He shook his head to settle his thoughts, willing away the surge of desire, the itching need in his fingertips to touch her cheek and savor the heat there. "Particularly from me."

She flinched a little. That had come out wrong.

"Not that you aren't lovely," he added hastily, with the sinking sensation that he only dug himself into a hole he wouldn't be able to talk himself out of. What about this girl flustered him so?

Besides that she looked like a faery out of an old tale, holding herself with queenly poise, even when her feathered charges rioted around her in unruly temper. "I just—I am, after all, married." Newly married, with a wife he should be lusting after instead of the goose girl.

"You would not be one to break your vows," she said, soft but steady.

She understood. Relieved, he nodded. "I would not. You can trust in that."

"It would be a horror to you," she ventured, "to compromise your integrity in such a way. That would undermine who you need to be, in order to rule wisely."

"Yes." Surprised at her insight, he wondered at it. "You're educated."

She blinked, then averted her gaze. "Not so much. After all—I didn't know to feed the geese."

An outright lie, but why? And she'd told Brenna she had no skills, as had Natilde. It wouldn't be unusual for a princess's waiting woman to be educated, possibly even noble, but it went beyond consideration that such a person would passively, even gratefully accept such a lowly position as goose girl. The job belonged to those like Conrad, who had little ability to learn more complex tasks. Surely Brenna could have seen Nix was no simpleton.

Perhaps she had. *An easy job to start, one that gets her out of the castle and gives her time with her thoughts.*

"Thank you." She curtseyed, clearly wanting him gone now. It felt like a dismissal, again not in keeping with a supposedly servile perspective. "I feel so terrible keeping you from your important duties."

Speaking of servicing. The primary duty that remained for

him squatted in the bridal chambers like a bejeweled toad. A terribly uncharitable thought and not one likely to make it easier to lay with his bride.

"It's fine," he told Nix, but didn't go. Didn't want to. He wanted to say something more, but didn't have words to define the feeling. For her part, Nix wound her fingers in her rough skirt looking, if anything, afraid. "If you need anything," he said slowly, following the impulse, "and you can't find me, just ask Brenna. She'll take care of you."

Nix nodded. "I'm doing fine. Your Highness. Don't worry about me."

"All right then. Good night." He left her, feeling as if he'd abandoned something important, and went to attend to his bride.

Natilde had donned a new gown for him. He knew this because she greeted him with the news, twirling and spinning to invite him to admire the details. Cavan hadn't had much occasion to observe ladies' fashion, but the gown seemed more worthy of a fancy ball or coronation than dinner in her rooms to be followed by heir-begetting. Not to mention the excessive amount of jewelry she'd donned to go with it. Still, mindful that he should be helping her feel cherished in her new home—for all their sakes—he put effort into praising the dress and flattering her beauty.

As usual, his father had given good advice because Natilde glowed at the attention, reveling in the courtly romantic gestures he offered. While they dined, she rattled on about the gowns she'd ordered, which seemed to be a staggeringly long list, considering she'd had a complete trousseau sent ahead, how they might compare to the styles worn by Her Highness, Princess Amelia, and how soon they could travel to Castle Ordnung, to pay their respects to the High Throne. The topics, however, allowed him to nod and listen, and—unfortunately—left him with entirely too much mental leisure to think of Nix and the mystery she posed.

Educated, he felt sure of it. More than that, she possessed a keen philosophical and political sense, that she contemplated questions of vows and honor, and that she noticed the details of how their kingdoms compared. Her hands, too—delicate bones, but with the roughness of chapped skin from the day's chores. Unaccustomed to manual work, which again meant a lady. Who was she really? It seemed clear she and Natilde had some sort of falling out. The more he grew to know each of them, the more it bothered him not to know exactly what had happened.

"I saw Nix a bit ago," he told Natilde after she finally wound down, watching her face for clues.

She looked blank. "Who?"

"Nix. Your waiting woman?"

Natilde frowned, then burst out laughing, unfortunately displaying her half-chewed meat. "Is that what she's calling herself? A fine joke, that."

"Why—what name do you know her by?"

Natilde clammed up, attempting to look innocent, but the expression didn't sit well on her. "I never knew her name. I didn't need to as she meant nothing to me. I told you to send her away. Where did you see her?"

"At the stables, when I returned my horse. She's caring for the geese, until we find a better occupation for her."

That sent Natilde into another round of laughter, so hearty she pressed her hands to her ribs. "She's the fucking goose girl? That is rich. I shall have to see that for myself. Far better for her to be my goose girl, yes, than to be sent away."

Her hilarity dug under his skin, but he mastered his irritation, less out of his resolve to be kinder to Natilde, than the pricking to solve the mystery of Nix. "She says she's content, so I agree."

That sobered Natilde immediately. "She spoke to you?"

Interesting. "Yes, both last night and this evening."

Natilde's mouth went ugly, tightening at the corners. "What did the little bitch say to you?"

His intuition went on high alert. People only asked that when they feared secrets might be spilled. "Oh, this and that. Nothing of import. Would you like more wine?"

Natilde held out her goblet, knuckles paling with her tense grip. Turbulent thoughts whirled behind her eyes and Cavan found himself waiting with great anticipation for what she'd say next, how she'd betray herself. For surely there was something here she didn't want him to know.

"You shouldn't consort with her ilk," Natilde finally said. "It lowers us all for you to be seen talking to servants. I have pride of place to maintain."

He had no reply to that. Certainly not one to please her. She did not yet know of his penchant for visiting Brenna, but he had no intention of severing that relationship, not even to keep the peace with his wife. It did, however, fit with what Nix had said about the formality of the court in Remus. Another difference between them to work around.

She read something of his reticence because she turned flirtatious and wheedling. "Come now, husband. Let's not fight. Take me to bed and let's see if we can't get that heir you long for."

Resigned to his duty, he sent for the maids to prepare the princess for bed. And thought about Nix, by way of readying his own self.

~ 7 ~

N IX VISITED FALADA before breakfast, soothing her grumpy mutters over the confinement. As a princess in the castle, she could have arranged special accommodations for Falada, even passing it off as a whim for a treasured steed. Now the best she could do was promise to bring her a treat from the kitchens. Mrs. Crocker happily offered some withered apples from her bin. Nix took them, then hesitated, thinking of Prince Cavan's suggestion.

"Mrs. Crocker?"

"Call me Brenna, child. No need to 'Mrs.' me."

Nix thought that wasn't true, but she knew little of the hierarchy among servants. Though she learned more of their world every day. A kingdom within a kingdom, complete with its own rulers, and she the least among them.

"Do you think… That is, Prince Cavan visited the stables last night and said I should ask you if I needed anything."

"Did he now?" Mrs. Crocker pursed her lips, sharp eyes surveying her. "He is, naturally, correct. Do I think what?"

"Would it be all right for me to take my horse out with the geese? So she gets some exercise?"

"Oh sure." Mrs. Crocker seemed surprised. "She's yours, isn't she?"

Nix hadn't been sure of that. Some held that servants could own nothing. "Thank you."

"No thanks needed. Here, I packed a lunch for you and Conrad. Should be a pretty day."

Conrad showed up at the stables just as Nix opened the doors to herd the geese out. "Where did you go?" he accused, yanking his staff out of her hand. "I went to the pond at dusk and you were gone."

"We found our own way back."

When he glared at her, she added, "I thought I heard a wolf howl and I was frightened."

That worked. Conrad squared his shoulders and puffed out his chest. "That's why you need me. Why is that horse here?"

"This is my horse, Falada. She's coming with us, for an outing."

"If she runs off, I'm not chasing after her."

"Fair enough," Nix agreed, suppressing her smile that the image of Falada leading Conrad on a merry chase. Falada nickered, something horsey that nevertheless sounded suspiciously like "idiot".

The day passed peacefully. The sun, when it finally tipped above the fog bank at the horizon, did shine prettily on the snowy trees and icy pond, a fanciful white glitter. Falada, loving the chance to stretch her legs, accompanied Nix on her walks around the lake, and they talked quietly—when Conrad wasn't near—of all they'd seen at their new home.

"We should leave this place," Falada insisted. "If not go home, then seek our fortunes elsewhere."

"But where and how? I've discovered I know nothing useful. At least here we have food and shelter." And Cavan. Though she could never claim him, she found herself unwilling to go far from him. Perhaps the intention she'd put behind her vows to him, marrying him in her heart and mind, though their marriage would remain forever unconsummated, colored how she felt. Perhaps something else drew her, as if the love she'd planned to give him pulled her along, no matter how she might resist. And then there was Princess Natilde, the beast Nix brought into the bosom of the kingdom and family who had acted to save Nix's own.

Nix sighed at the thought of setting out, frustrated with her own timidity, but also afraid of what worse might happen. She needed to shake this feeling that she should stay near Cavan. "I'll think about it. Maybe when the weather warms."

"I have a bad feeling that—"

Falada broke off when Conrad approached, seeing him with her wider peripheral vision, as he yet again stole up on Nix to snatch a strand of her hair. He'd formed an obsession with it and had already plucked several hairs, to Nix's growing annoyance. This time Falada pretended to stumble, knocking the boy aside. He took off in a fury, once again leaving Nix to bring the geese home herself. Which suited her just fine as she and Falada could speak freely and relax without eavesdropping ears and the bites of pulled hair.

Her peaceful mood evaporated when they entered the inner yard and the princess swept out from the main doors, elaborate skirts swishing, jewels glittering colder than the ice of the pond, as she made straight for Nix. Sweat popped out on her temples, chilling on her skin, and nausea gripped her stomach. The princess knew it and smiled cruelly, though she stayed clear of the geese, several of whom hissed and tried to nip her.

"How the mighty have fallen," Natilde sneered. "A goose girl. Abase yourself before your betters."

Her legs weak and trembling, Nix released Falada's halter and knelt in the muddy slush, the geese standing tall around her.

"I hear you've been *talking*." Natilde nudged her shoulder with a pointed shoe, the brightly expensive embroidery soiled. "But that would be stupid."

"Yes, Princess Natilde." She shivered and hated herself for being so afraid. So weak and worthless.

"Yes, you've been talking?"

"Your Highness—I've only spoken of small, daily things, so as not to be rude to my betters. Nothing of import."

"Keep it that way. Remember who has the power now. Or do you and I need to take a little walk, so I can remind you?"

"I remember. I won't say a thing. I promise." Though she hated herself for it, she shook with fear at the cruel green gleam of the woman's eyes, her skin crawling with the memory of those nails biting into her, the slices of the knife blade, the helplessness rising up to choke her.

"I'd have your throat slit now if it didn't please me so to see you brought so low. The prince loves me—practically worships me—and after we fuck like bunnies we sit and laugh about how pitiful you are, how you are less than nothing."

Nix said nothing, just wanting the confrontation done, the chill seeping through her skirts. Though her erstwhile serving woman wouldn't realize how she contradicted herself, to insist that Nix was both insignificant and worthy of discussing with the prince. Truly, it gave Nix warning, that the woman would never cease fearing the truth. She couldn't stay and hope to live. Nor could she protect Falada. The faery was right that they should leave.

"My lady wife?" Cavan's voice rang across the yard and Nix groaned to herself in despair, mortified that he should witness this. Terrified that he'd make things worse. Everything rested on him never knowing. Or even giving the appearance of coming close to the truth. If the princess even suspected…

He strode up. "What goes on here?"

"I'm disciplining this servant," the princess replied, in a haughty tone. "She stole a horse from the stables."

"Isn't that Nix's horse—the one she rode here?"

"Both horses are mine. A goose girl owns nothing. She should be lashed."

A silent pause made Nix risk glancing up. Prince Cavan wore a neutral expression, but his gray eyes had gone harder than stone. An honorable man and a gentle one—but no pushover, no fool. Danger crackled in the air, though his voice remained smooth. "The king decides all punishments."

"Then I shall speak to him."

"A fine idea. Let me escort you inside, lest you take a chill." When Natilde didn't budge, he picked up her hand, swept her a gallant bow and kissed it. "After all, you may already bear our child. We cannot risk such a precious burden."

She softened and smiled, allowing the prince to cajole her with flattery as he led her back into the castle, leaving Nix to pick herself up from the mud, her skirts soaked through.

"If your mother only knew—"

"Don't say it. Don't speak at all, or she will find out." Nix fought the wave of exhaustion that swamped her as her terror ebbed back into dull dread. She handed Falada off to a stable lad and slowly made her way to the goose pen. With no Conrad in sight, she fetched the grain and scattered it for her birds, following Cavan's example and singing to them as she did, trying to soothe both them and herself with the trickle of magic, despite her chattering teeth and the shivers that wracked her body. As much from terror of the looming consequences as cold.

The pen door opened, making her start, and Cavan stepped in, closing it behind him. His fury showed plainly now in the steely glare he leveled on her. So handsome in the imposing force of his personality, the inherent nobility of his character. "What in the Twelve was that about?" he demanded.

Her heart fluttered at his harsh tone and she quailed, unable to withstand any more, fighting the urge to fling herself against his strong body for comfort.

As if reading her mind, Cavan cursed and waded through the feeding geese, taking her by the arms. "Don't cringe like that. I'm not mad at you. Look at you—you're soaked to the bone and shivering. Why didn't you change into warmer clothes?"

"Th-th—the g-g-geese," she got out between chattering teeth.

He looked incredulous. "Danu take the geese!" Taking the bucket of grain, he upended it and tossed it down. "Where is your room—through here?"

Answering his own question, the prince pulled her into her little room, turning his back to light her brazier of coals. "Get undressed and under the blankets. I won't look."

Almost too numb to move, she hesitated and he threw her a ferocious glance. "Move, Nix."

Fumbling with the ties and catches, taking down her hair for extra warmth, she obeyed, sliding gratefully under the pile of blankets, frozen to the bone.

FORTUNATELY, NIX SAVED him having to strip her out of those

soaked clothes, rustling as she undressed and climbed into her bed. It didn't save him picturing her slim, delicate body in all her naked glory, but it helped calm the fury that had gripped him at the sight of her kneeling in icy muck, white and terrified, as Natilde berated her.

"Are you covered?" He asked, setting her little teapot on the grate to boil.

"Y-yes."

He set his teeth at the sound of hers chattering. Taking a deep breath, he turned to find her tucked in the corner of her bed, dwarfed by the mound of blankets pulled up around her so only her piquant face showed, framed by the fall of her ivory hair. Sitting beside her, he chaffed her arms through the covers. "I'm brewing tea for you. You'll drink it and then you'll tell me what is going on between you and Princess Natilde."

Her enormous blue eyes darkened and swam with tears she didn't shed. "Your Highness—please, no. There's nothing to know. The princess was simply angry that I took her horse. I won't do it again."

That wasn't it. Obviously it wasn't, as Natilde hadn't given a moment's thought to the horses since she arrived. "Talk to me, Nix. I can't help you if you don't tell me the truth."

"That is the truth."

"You're lying to me. So is she. Why?"

"Please, Cavan." Nix leaned in beseeching him, seeming unaware that she'd used his name so familiarly. "You can help me by leaving me alone. You shouldn't be here, talking to me."

"You seem to forget that this is my castle, my kingdom and—after my father and the High King—only I decide what I shouldn't do."

She jerked back, a frustrated refusal that revealed a surprising glint of temper. The movement caused a lock of her hair to fall across his hand, a sensuous glide of silk. He wrapped it around his finger, somehow unable to help himself, mesmerized by the almost magical whiteness of it against his sun-darkened skin, the seductive texture. She made a small sound and he dragged his gaze up. Staring at him with emotion stark on her face, she filled him with a tide of longing he could no longer resist. Moving slowly, feeling like he walked in a dream, as if he knew her from those dreams, he slid his other hand behind her slender neck, urging her closer, brushing her mouth with his.

Cool and petal-soft, her lips yielded, then parted, allowing him into the startling fire within. He deepened the kiss, starving for more, and she moaned, pressing into him. She tasted of spring, how pink rosebuds look trembling against a blue morning, and she fit against him in a way that made him feel both fiercely protective and desperate to pull the blankets away, to stroke her naked skin into heat.

But she tore her mouth away, pushing against his chest with surprising fierceness, so that the covers fell off her dainty shoulders. "No, you can't!" She stared him down, full of regal command. "Think, Cavan. You promised."

He'd promised not to touch her. Cursing himself, he rubbed his face. "I'm sorry, Nix. I didn't mean to frighten you."

"No." She fought a hand out from under the blankets and laid it on his knee. Only she could go from chastising to comforting in a flash. "You didn't. You never could. But your honor, your wedding vows—you can't do this. You would never forgive yourself."

He took her hand in his, trying not to look at how the blanket fell away from her bare shoulder, revealing the hint of the upper curve of her breast. If only he felt a shadow of this desire for his wife. A woman he grew to despise more with every passing hour. "How is it honorable of me to succor a woman—I don't care about her bloodlines—who can treat someone else so viciously?"

"Because she is your lawful wife," Nix said, with gentle implacability. "She will be your queen and you are too noble, too good of a man and a prince to treat her as anything but that."

"I don't know if I can do it, Nix," he surprised himself by confessing, wanting nothing more than to lay his head in her lap and rest there a while.

As if she sensed it, she let go his hand and ran cool fingers over his brow, sliding them through his hair. "You can do anything. I believe in you. Two kingdoms depend on you, my prince. At least, Remus does. Princess Natilde—she made the journey here, marrying a man she'd never met, entirely to save the people of Remus. If you can't love her, love them. They need you."

"They have Queen Isyn still."

"Yes, but she is very ill. Far more so than she wants anyone to know. Some of the lesser nobles are greedy and, with her not being able to hold court as often or as long, they take advantage. Not all the starvation is due to crops ruined by flooding. Not all the deaths are due to disease. Food and supplies are diverted, sold elsewhere to line corrupt pockets."

He contemplated that, surprised at Nix's perception and knowledge. "The queen knows this?"

"Yes. Or she would not have married off her only child to gain the protection of the Twelve. Erie is not only the closest kingdom to ours, but King Wyn has a reputation for fairness and putting the welfare of the people before all else. She's counting on him seeing through the corruption quickly and cleaning it away. Something she lacks the strength to do, surrounded as she is by those seeking only to use her."

He studied her. She looked so lovely, a white flame in the shadowed stable, calm and steady, her trembling fear forgotten in considering the problems of her former home. But hadn't Natilde called her a foreigner? Something very odd there. "How do you, a mere servant, know all of this?"

She pressed her fingers to her mouth, eyes going wide. Then shrugged and picked at the blanket. "Servants gossip. Do you think Mrs. Crocker doesn't know everything that goes on in the castle, if not in all of Marcellum?"

"True. You are wise beyond your years."

She blushed, long ivory lashes like ever-frozen lacy snow-flakes against her cheekbones as she kept her gaze down. It made him want to lift her chin, so she'd look at him again. So he could kiss her until she melted, but she was right. He could not betray his own self, his promises to his father, king and both their kingdoms, no matter his personal feelings. Turning his head, he pressed a kiss to Nix's palm. Then resolutely moved away from her.

"You're right, of course. I'm fortunate to have you be my moral compass, since I seem to have lost my way."

"Not lost." She smiled, but wounded grief lurked behind it. "Sometimes we are knocked off our road and need another to help us up again."

"What is your road, Nix?" He hadn't meant to ask it—and regretted the impulse even more when her expression darkened further.

"I don't know. I think—I think maybe I have to leave here, to find it again."

The thought of her departure stabbed him with a sense of

panic. "No," he said, too sharply. Reeled himself back. "I mean, not in such brutal weather. The distances are long between towns here and you would suffer from the lack of shelter. Wait until spring and, if you still want to go, I'll see to it that you have supplies and an escort."

A laugh quivered on her pretty mouth. "An escort for a goose girl? That would be a sight to see."

He smiled back, though he didn't feel it in his heart. "If you want to go back to Remus, you could travel with the troops and supplies we'll be sending."

She looked thoughtful. "Perhaps I could. Not back to Queen Isyn's palace, but…elsewhere."

"Promise me you won't go yet."

She shook her head, hair falling around her lowered face like a bridal veil. "I can't promise that."

"Then promise you won't leave without telling me, without giving me the opportunity to see you're safely supplied and protected." He didn't care if it made rational sense or not—he wouldn't be able to live with himself if he didn't do all he could for her.

"All right," she said in a soft voice, still not looking at him. "I promise not to leave without telling you. Now promise me you'll go now and never tell Princess Natilde anything of this. Swear on my life."

"On your life?" He smiled at her, trying to tease an answering smile from her, but she only regarded him gravely. "All right then, I swear."

"Thank you," she answered softly and it seemed to him she said something else behind the words.

He left her, knowing it to be the right and honorable thing, wondering why a sense of terrible foreboding plagued him.

$$\sim 8 \sim$$

FALADA'S SCREAM OF fury woke Nix from a dream of sweet kisses and warm springtime. Fervently grateful she'd dressed again in dry clothes, she flung herself through the honking, spitting geese, threw open the gates to the pen and ran towards the sounds. The geese poured out after her, an enraged escort for her headlong rush to the source of Falada's cries.

Which went abruptly silent.

A sob lodging in her chest, compressing her heart so it could not beat, she rounded the corner of the back part of the stables. Where the knacker worked in a pool of blood, finishing the job of ending Falada's life.

A high keening filled her head, echoing against her skull, and the knacker glanced up in shock. Then rushed to catch her as she swayed in an onrushing faint, smearing her sleeves with fresh blood.

Falada's blood.

Falada was dead.

It couldn't be.

"Oh dearie," he said kindly. "This is not a sight for a young girl. Sometimes it must be done, but it's not for all to see. Look away."

She couldn't. All the world narrowed to one searing truth.

Her final, excruciating failure. She'd failed Falada. The least she could do was force herself to look.

"Wh—why?" She gasped past the blade in her heart.

The knacker's voice came from the end of a long tunnel. "She seemed to be a fine horse, yes, but Princess Natilde worried at her vicious nature. Once a horse turns mean, becomes a biter, they can be a danger to all."

Nix laughed, a hysterical cackle that made the man flinch. *Natilde.* The hated name, once hers and now all that oozed evil in her world, hissed through her brain. Not enough for her to win, the woman had to destroy. She wouldn't rest until she'd robbed Nix of everything that mattered. And Nix had let her.

Enough of this.

A memory of her mother rode the wild burst of hatred. The ailing queen taking the sharp knife, cutting her finger, the drops of heart's blood falling, staining the white cambric. Heart's blood, shed in sacrifice to protect her daughter. She could do no less for Falada.

She grabbed hold of the knacker, whose kind eyes went white around the edges in apprehension. "Will you do something for me?" She demanded. Not asking, not really. Phrasing it as a question but infusing it with all the royal command she possessed.

"Of—of course," he stammered, a man willing to promise anything to escape the hysterical crazy woman. "If I can."

"You can," she assured him, reinforcing the directive. "Did Prin—did *she* tell you to hang the head somewhere?"

"Yes—" He looked from side to side, seeking an answer. "How did you know?"

"Where?"

"Over the gate that leads to the goose pond. I don't know

why."

Nix knew why. "I will meet you there to watch. Don't do it before I get there."

He frowned, confused, and worked at removing her hands from his bloodied apron. "All right. If it will please you, I can't see as it would do any harm."

"You'll do it now, while her blood is fresh. I'll gather my geese."

Clearly willing to do anything to get her to leave, he agreed. Nix turned away from the sight of Falada's broken corpse and, raging grief blackening her thoughts, she set to rounding up the geese. When Conrad showed and began complaining that the geese had run loose, she turned and hissed at him, like one of her charges. He blanched, taking in the blood stains on her hands and clothes, and backed off, meekly assisting and following her bidding.

By the time they made it to the gate, the knacker waited with a ladder and Falada's head steaming still in the frosty air. He seemed anxious to get it over with, but she made him wait a moment longer.

Casting her mind back to her mother's chamber, to the day she sent Nix away to a marriage that would never be, she tore a bit of fabric from her cuff where Falada's blood stained it bright and crimson. Pricking her finger with a knife as her mother had done, she sang an old song under her breath.

Heart's blood to calm you.
Heart's blood to keep you.
Heart's blood to live on in me.

She went to Falada's head and, with resolve she'd never expected she possessed, tucked the bloody fabric deep in her mouth. Nodding to the knacker, she stepped back. "You may proceed."

Wild-eyed, he worked quickly, hauling the head up the ladder and nailing it in place, muttering some prayer as he did. A pool of sticky blood formed in the snow beneath. Conrad stood a ways off, face contorted in astonished disgust. Nix waited for the knacker to leave, the magic pounding through her heart, answering the call of blood. Hoping enough of Falada's magical spirit remained nearby.

"Alas! dear Falada, there thou hangest," she whispered.

The head opened its eyes, coated milky white with death. "Alas! Queen's daughter, there thou gangest." The voice came out thready, uneven. "If thy mother knew thy fate, her heart would break with grief so great."

Conrad made a strangled sound of terror, threw down his staff. It fell in the puddle of coagulating blood as he raced back to the castle and Nix picked it up, smearing the polished wood with Falada's faerie magic. It wound with her own and coalesced, the steam of fading death forming into a shape, until the horse's ghost stood beside her.

"Ready to watch the geese?" she asked and headed down the road, Falada's ghost trotting alongside. No greetings from the folks she passed on her way that morning. Instead they offered rolling glances of horror and concern for her blood-spattered self. She ignored them, singing a jaunty tune, Falada carrying the harmony.

They spent a pleasant day, though the clouds gathered and snow began to fall, growing denser by the hour. Over and over, Nix told Falada how sorry she was that she'd balked at leaving and the ghost swirled the snowflakes in a dance to lighten Nix's grief.

She didn't want to be cozened, however. Instead she clung

to the boiling fury, forging her black devastation into shining rage. Carefully she fed it with every bit of heart magic, of the fear, the despair, the debilitating weakness she felt, nurturing it like the babes she would never bear. She could never be Cavan's wife in truth, could not devastate his noble heart with the knowledge that he'd been duped, had violated his marriage vows and defiled his body. But she could set him free. Natilde had killed herself when she spoke Falada's death warrant. Nix would simply be her executioner. She'd die gladly for the crime. Perhaps her ghost could join Falada's, circling the goose pond for eternity.

With Natilde and Nix both dead, Cavan could marry again. Perhaps to a woman he could like better, one who'd be a good queen for their combined kingdoms. Something she hadn't considered until she passed along what Cavan needed to know. Natilde's personal corruption rivaled even the worst of the nobles.

Entirely possible they'd sent her on purpose, planning to have her take Nix's place all along.

If so, they would not succeed in that, either. The widowed Cavan would retain rule over both kingdoms—and he'd know what he faced. His children, the progeny of one of the best men she'd ever met, would take the throne someday. Perhaps they'd visit the pond in springtime and she could make the petals of the cherry blossoms dance for them, to tease out their laughter.

Once this was done, there should be laughter to fill the holes.

A sharp nip on her cheek jolted her out of her brooding thoughts, the geese pressing around her in anxiety, flapping their clipped wings to send the snowflakes spinning. She'd waited overlong, the sky dark and snow deep around her. She wasn't cold, though. Instead a drowsy warmth infused her. The blaze of revenge. Savoring it, she tipped her face to the sky, letting the snowflakes slide off the forged heat of her skin.

SNOW FELL AROUND Cavan, so densely that he almost couldn't make out the grotesque sight.

But there it hung, the head of Nix's horse, nailed above the gate to the town road, just as Conrad had told Brenna. The boy had spun a wild tale of a blood-spattered, wild-eyed Nix talking to the head and the dead flesh speaking back in archaic rhymes. Brenna called Conrad more daft than usual, but the knacker—poor thrice-damned man—verified that Natilde had demanded he hang the head there, and Nix had done… something to it. She'd been crazed, he said, and he'd been rattled to begin with, imagining that the horse had begged him not to kill her.

Strange events that chilled Cavan more than the snow soaking through his cloak. Not the least of which was the horror of Natilde, ordering the horse's death, having it hung where Nix would see it. Another escalation of her mysterious vendetta against Nix. One abhorrent to both his own nature and the values set by the king. No life should be wasted thus. Frost rimmed the once-elegant ears and snow furred over lashes, closed against the mare's fine-boned eye sockets. She had been a fine horse. Worse than a crime to have carelessly destroyed her.

Or deliberately. For surely this had wounded Nix unbearably.

His mind reeled at how to handle this, what to say to his wife, when he wanted most to wrap his hands around her slender, bejeweled throat and enjoy the glee of seeing the life fade from her poisonous gaze.

Also revolting, how much he wanted that. Values be thrice-dammed.

As he moved beneath the head, a trick of the light or the falling snow made it seem as if the horse's muzzle flexed, lips drawing back. The hiss of wind carried a voice, female and full of sorrow. *Her heart would break…*

A chill that had nothing to do with the weather raised the hairs on his neck and spurred him through the gate and down the deserted road. Muscles straining as he broke trail in the deepening snow, he focused on finding Nix. She should have returned hours since. Wretched Conrad, telling no one he'd left her out there alone. Napping in the stables until Brenna rousted him out. Cavan could have sent men to fetch her—probably should have brought some along—but he'd been too impatient. And haunted by the dread that he'd somehow caused this. It fell to him to find Nix and bring her home. Brenna, with a searching glance and a shrewd nod, hadn't tried to talk him out of it.

He nearly missed the turn-off to the pond, the snow had covered it so fully. But the sound of a goose honking had him turning back. The lone goose shook off its cape of snow and, hissing at him, flapped its waddling way down the snowy bank. Cavan sank to mid-thigh, struggling through, fearing for Nix more than ever. Only a gaggle of the birds milled about on the verge, scuffling snowflakes into wild patterns with their wings. No sign of Nix.

In the pattern of falling snow, it seemed a horse pranced. A wraith of mist there and gone. With nothing else to go on, he followed it.

And nearly fell over Nix.

Buried in snow, surrounded by milling geese, she looked as dead as the mare's ghost. As erased as her name implied. Her skin and hair white as bone, she seemed a sculpture made of the snow lovingly piled upon her. But when he strangled out her name, her frozen lashes fluttered, and she opened eyes the color of high summer sky.

With a curse, Cavan gathered her up, snow shedding from her cloak to reveal more colors. Wading through the drifts, the brassy honks of geese echoing his straining heart, he regretted not having more help. This was his penance then, for whatever of his failures had made this come to pass.

Nix watched him, eyes guileless as a doll's and—once or twice—their glassy quality made him think she too had died. But her gaze remained fixed on his, her bloodless lips moving in some soundless song or prayer. When they passed beneath the mare's severed head, intelligence moved behind the deep blue glass. And something else.

Fury.

He took the back way, the servants' entrance directly to the warm kitchens. Several maids shrieked at the sight of him and one dropped a tray of bread to make the Circle of Glorianna. Brenna wasted no time pointing out that this was their prince and no ghost or frost-monster, and set them to work rescuing the bread and boiling more water.

When she turned to lead the way to the stables, Cavan shook his head, melting snow falling in runnels down his neck, shedding around him like a surge of spring run-off. Instead he climbed the servants' stairs, two, three at a time and carried Nix to his own chambers. Brenna barred the door behind them and fixed him with a worried frown.

"You can't have the girl here," she fretted. "It's not done and—"

"Am I not a prince? Heir to the throne and penultimate ruler of all in Erie?" He ground out the words in a voice that made Brenna widen her eyes in trepidation. He'd failed to act before and would not make that mistake again. "I decide what is done. Only the king can countermand."

Heedless of the snow soaking her, he set Nix on his great bed. She watched him with those vacant blue eyes as he fumbled with frozen fingers at the ties of her cloak. Not without compassion, Brenna shouldered in and took over the work, briskly bidding him to turn his back and change his own garments as she efficiently stripped Nix of her clothes and tucked her under the covers. When he returned, she'd taken away the sodden coverlet and whisked out another goose-down comforter.

Brenna searched his face, hands fisted on her hips. "What is this about, Cavan?"

He looked past her to Nix, ivory hair spread over the white pillows to dry. A porcelain doll, shattered by brutality. He swallowed down his guilt to force out the words. "I'm in love with her."

"Oh, my sweet boy." Brenna whispered in devastation, then clutched his arm, forcing him to look at her. "That cannot be. You will ruin her and the Princess will use this to destroy you both. Your marriage is too new. You don't yet have an heir. Think of your duty to—"

"I'm sick to death of a duty that forces me to bed a woman I loathe and to turn my back on someone who deserves my protection." He said it forcefully enough that Brenna, shocked, released him and stepped back. "What kind of man am I," he asked her more gently, "what kind of king would I be, if I turn away from what I know in my heart to be right, to embrace a surface that covers a vile wrong? This is the right thing to do—I know it in my heart."

She scrubbed her hands in her apron. "All right then. How do you want to handle this, my Prince?"

"One step at a time." Impulsively, he hugged her, as he hadn't in years, since he'd grown into a man. "She must live before we can do aught else."

"She'll live." Brenna patted his back, her voice watery. "She's far tougher than she seems. I'll bring the things and keep this quiet. But remember—I can keep everyone out but the king. You're on your own there."

"I'll handle my father, if it comes to that." He'd find a way.

He barred the door behind Brenna and returned to sit with Nix. A hint of rose had enlivened her lips, the sweet line of her cheekbones, but she stared into nothing. Her mouth moved, repeating words he could not hear. Bending closer, he put an ear to her lips, the chill emanating from her as from the walls of ice in the north.

The words hissed together, tangling and blurred, until he made them out, bit by bit, and strung them together. "Alas! dear Falada, there thou hangest." Over and over.

He called her name, stroking her cheek, but she seemed not to hear him, buried in her prayer. Except it sounded less reverent or supplicating, and more like a witch's chant. A thread of rage and revenge wound through the simple words that stirred his own blood, prodded and compelled him.

So much so that, when Brenna returned with her supplies, he swung on his own cloak again and—shushing her protests— went out into the storm.

The mare's head, hung there still, the shroud of snow doing little to disguise its ghastly impact. Steeling himself, he repeated Nix's words. "Alas! dear Falada, there thou hangest."

Ice glittered in the air, along with a potent surge of a magic he'd never encountered but recognized instantly. It sounded blue as Nix's haunted gaze and smelled of spring rain. Frost shattered off the severed head as its eyes opened, the burning white glare of its dead eyes riveting him.

And spoke.

"Alas! Queen's daughter, there thou gangest. If thy mother knew thy fate, her heart would break with grief so great."

The words tolled through him, a broken bell of warning, sinking him to his knees. Much as Nix had cowered before Natilde. No—Nix was the Princess Natilde. Which meant the woman in the bridal chamber, the one he'd bedded… was someone else, entirely. He'd betrayed his wedded wife, his vows.

To Nix. Who'd known the truth and hadn't said.

It would be a horror to you to compromise your integrity in such a way. That would undermine who you need to be.

What did the little bitch say to you?

You shouldn't consort with her ilk.

He'd been duped. Tricked. And stupid.

~ 9 ~

THE WARMTH OF soup and kind words penetrated her icy shell. Goose down surrounded her and, for a dreamy space, Nix imagined the geese had wrapped her up in their wings, keeping her warm and safe.

As if they too had thawed, tears melted down her face and Brenna tutted, wiping them away. Focusing on the woman's kind, concerned face, Nix tried to think where she might be.

"You're in Prince Cavan's bedchambers," Brenna told her and fed her a spoonful of soup. "He found you in the snow and brought you back."

That explained the great bed, the carved wooden posts and elaborately inlaid fireplace, heating the room with life-giving flames. Not her cozy room in the stables. Where she belonged. A goose girl, not a princess.

"I shouldn't be here," she whispered to no one.

"Your Prince put you here, so I imagine that means you should be," Brenna returned with confidence. But she didn't entirely believe her own words. She sounded worried. Concerned for the man she loved like her own.

"Where is Cavan?"

Brenna pressed her lips together and shook her head. "You don't worry about that. Your job is to eat soup, drink tea and rest. Everything else will come as it will."

As if summoned by her words, a fist pounded on the doors, spurring her heart into a similar thudding rhythm. Brenna rose, checked the peephole, and unbarred it. Cavan burst into the chamber, snow falling away from his cloak like feathers, gray eyes like stormclouds as they fixed on her. He looked wild, like a warrior from an old tapestry, as if he should be swinging a great sword on a battlefield. "Leave us," he snapped at Brenna, never taking his gaze off Nix.

Far from taking offense at his brusque order, Brenna smiled and bobbed a curtsy. "See that she keeps eating."

Wanting to beg the woman not to leave her with this man she wanted so badly and dared not claim, Nix shrank into the covers as he barred the door, locking her in. If only the goose down could swallow her up and bury her. But Cavan's steel-sharp glare kept her pinned to the world. He dropped his cloak to the floor and strode to her, stripping off his gloves as he came. One knee brought him up onto the bed and he bracketed her face in his hands, holding her still for his questioning.

"Why didn't you tell me who you are, Princess Natilde?"

The question knifed through her. "Don't call me that."

"It's who you are."

"No."

"No?" His hands tightened on her face. "Don't you lie to me. You've lied enough."

"It's not a lie. I never lied. I'm not her anymore." She managed to get her arms from under the swaddling covers, wrapped her fingers around his strong wrists, not to pull them away, but to hold on. So she wouldn't go under. "I lost her. Maybe I never had a good grip on her to begin with, but I left her on an icy stream bank and I can't ever be her again." As if the shell had been ripped from her along with her clothes, leaving a small and naked thing. All the wrong size.

"You are the woman I married, that I exchanged vows with. Not the other."

"I'm sorry," she whispered, willing him to understand. "I'm so, so sorry. I hoped you'd never find out."

"Why?" He looked so bleakly confounded, lost as she'd been. "If only you'd told me, I would never have bedded another, violating my vows to you."

"But you didn't," she insisted. "You operated out of the best of intentions, so there is no stain upon you for it."

"There *is*." His fingers dug into her cheekbones in a way that made her want to weep, not from pain, but from his anguished scrutiny that laid her bare. "I failed you, in the worst possible way."

"Cavan…no." She leaned in, willing him to understand. "I failed. I couldn't seem to stop any of it. I let her strip me, h— hurt me. Take my place in your bed. Take Falada from me. There wasn't anything I could do."

"You could have told me."

"I couldn't. It's a terrible thing to discover that you are nothing. Why would you have believed me? I had no proof." Her throat clenched around the final confession. "I am no longer a virgin, Cavan."

His brow grew thunderous. "You were raped? Who? I'll have him flayed for this."

"No man. *She* did it. With the hilt of a knife." The dismay in his face sickened her. "I'm so sorry."

"Ah, Nix." His grip slackened and he slid fingers into her hair, drawing them through, much as she might have with Falada's mane. She closed her eyes against the memory. "All this time," he murmured, "I wondered how I could be so drawn to you, why I felt a connection to you and not her."

"I feel it, too. The vows, perhaps," she said, his touch making her both sleepy and roused.

"What do you mean?"

"As if, by promising ourselves, even far apart as we were, we connected. We both wanted to do what's right for our people. I see that in you, the way I know it in myself."

"I knew you, also, in my heart, from dreams or another place. But it's more than that. From the first moment, and adding on with each moment after, I fell in love with you." His voice came hoarse as his hands drifted over her shoulders, tracing her collarbones. Her nipples peaked and she became aware that the covers had fallen away and she sat bare-breasted before him. Cavan's gaze followed her thought and his hands. "I thought of you, all the while. Pretended it was your skin I touched, your thighs I spread."

"Then it was."

His eyes rose to hers, dubious, still anguished, but with heat burning through, an equinox of the heart, turning and tripping the season between them.

"The intention of the mind carries more weight than the action of the body," she told him, remembering her mother explaining that very thing. Which hadn't made sense then. Now it did. "You kept your vows to me, Cavan. It was me you made love to. Me who you consecrated to your heart. I have been your wife all along."

"Then you are still virgin, by that reasoning. You never betrayed me with another, not in your heart or mind. But Nix— that part never mattered to me. More than anything, I wanted a queen, a worthy partner, the one who understands the people and acts to do what's best for them. You, my queen." He said it with reverence, placing a kiss on her forehead.

"And your goose girl," she smiled a little to herself at that. The wintery grief, the freezing rage subsided some, making her think perhaps the clouds would part and spring would come again. "Would you lie with me in truth, Cavan? Make flesh of our bonds."

He pulled back to search her face. "Are you sure? You said she hurt you."

Oh yes, the cruel violation. The taunting and brutality. She wanted it gone. "Let's erase her from both of our bodies, wash her taint away and forge our connection anew."

Cavan groaned as she touched him in return, parting his shirt, stroking his burning skin. "Now? You're grief-stricken, nearly froze to death…" He lost the words when she pressed her lips to the hollow at the base of his throat.

"Yes. Bring me back to life, my Prince, flesh of my flesh."

As if unable to help himself, his hands went to her breasts, cupping them as he might china teacups. The heat penetrated into her body from them, infusing her heart with hope, with a greater fire. She dropped her head back, arching into him. This was real. She came to him a virgin still, because nothing that had happened before had been like this. He lowered his mouth to kiss her nipples and she ran fingers through his dark hair, moving under his lips, allowing the magic of desire to fill her veins, suffusing her with a power she'd never known.

"Nix," he murmured against her skin and it felt good and right. She'd found herself in nothingness and, like a seed planted in soil, grew from that, unfurling leaf by leaf, soon to blossom.

"Yes," she answered, pushing the covers aside so he'd see all of her. He took her in, the admiration in his eyes a balm to all her wounds. She knelt up to ease his shirt from his shoulders, to run her hands over his muscled shoulders and lean chest, the feel of his skin like sparkling magic. When she had him naked, she lay back, pulling him with her, spreading her thighs so he'd come between them where she needed him.

"Not yet," he murmured. "Let me undo what she did. Show me how she hurt you."

"I can't." She shrank away from the jagged memories.

"You can. Show me."

"I…I hit my head on the ice."

"Where?"

"Here."

He kissed her forehead, sending warmth into her, as if thawing the ice that had knocked her nearly senseless. Bit by bit, he covered her skin with kisses, murmuring love and comfort over each of the old bruises, the healing cuts. Her tortured nipples received lavish attention that went to her core, turning chill to heat. At last, at her whispered confession, he settled his mouth between her legs. She cried out at the utter pleasure of it, winding her fingers in his dark hair.

This was how it should be. The two of them, coming together like their kingdoms. Healing all.

They cried out together when he finally sheathed himself in her and a deep vibration, like a faraway gong rang through the foundations of both their kingdoms. Finally joined, the land shivered and settled in her mind and heart, flowing from him to her, into the earth and back again.

Not far away, Falada murmured her approval. Still there, as always.

<h1 style="text-align:center">~ 10 ~</h1>

CAVAN HANDED NATILDE into the throne beside his, then seated himself. She would take the name with her to her fate, as Nix wanted no part of it. After hearing her story, he couldn't blame her at all. Much as he felt on edge, he forced himself to appear at ease. Only partially successfully, as the King gave him a curious nod and waved a hand to indicate formal court had begun.

Much would depend on what King Wyn perceived and decided.

"Send the first petitioner," he proclaimed.

The great doors to the hall opened and Nix, in a gown of white feathers, ivory hair streaming down her back, walked up the aisle toward him. She kept her gaze fixed on him, showing only a hint of her old timidity. Otherwise, she shimmered with power. More people than he glimpsed the ghost of Falada proudly prancing behind her, for a susurrus of whispers ran through the assembly, a tone of wonder and awe.

Beside him, Natilde shifted, a choking sound in the back of her throat. Good. She should be afraid.

"Who comes before me?" King Wyn intoned. Not truly a question, but to set the record.

"Nix, the Goose Girl."

"And what wrong do you seek to redress?"

"Against the traitor and imposter claiming to be Princess Natilde." Righteous anger infused her voice, filling a hall gone abruptly silent in shock. All eyes swung to the throne beside him.

King Wyn straightened slowly and Cavan watched him in trepidation, half-afraid he'd dismiss her out of hand. But whatever his faults, Wyn was a fair and honest king. Nix had been right about that—and her reasoning sound for handling this in open court. He would hear her out as he would any of the least of his subjects.

Flicking an oblique look that assessed his son's calm demeanor, Wyn agreed. "State your case."

"The woman on the throne masqueraded as a waiting woman and attacked the Princess Natilde on the journey here, causing her great harm and forcing her to trade places, bedding Prince Cavan in her stead."

The court remained thrummingly silent, no one stirring lest they miss a word of the scandalous news.

"Lies!" Natilde cried out. "This servant, this goose girl, is a viper to my heart. Yes, she tried to take my place on the journey here, but I fought her off. I've tried to be tolerant. I thought to let her live, but I cannot sit here and allow her to spew her vile poison in this court. Execute her immediately." As King Wyn leveled a simmering glare upon her, she added, "I mean, so I advise you, my King. Look at her—she is clearly unhinged."

"None other than the petitioner may speak." He turned his attention back to Nix. "Have you any proof of this claim, goose girl?"

"No, King Wyn. I do not." She held herself regally, unapologetic.

"And do you claim to be Princess Natilde, in her stead?"

Some whispering giggles in the court now, scoffing at the possibility. His Nix did not flinch. She'd survived far worse. "I do not."

Wyn seemed surprised, glancing again at his son. "No? Then where is she?"

"Left behind as our childhood selves inevitably are. I am Queen Isyn's daughter, heir to Remus, wife to Cavan, pledged to be the future Queen of Erie."

"And yet you have no proof."

Cavan edged forward, but his father held up a warning hand to forestall him. Nix seemed icily composed, but she looked to him briefly a glint of nerves in her deep blue gaze.

"Only this. There are those who stand to benefit from disrupting the union of our kingdoms. Perhaps a search of her things will reveal who she colludes with to undermine both your throne and my mother's. Also…" She firmed her chin. "Prince Cavan knows who I am."

"Cavan!" The erstwhile Natilde hissed out. "How can you sit there and say nothing? I am your wife, who you lawfully bedded." The threat implicit in her tone rustled through the room.

Wyn looked to him. "Yes, Cavan—what say you?"

He settled his gaze on Nix, knowing their connection, to each other and the land. "I know Nix behaves as a queen should. I say search Natilde's rooms. If necessary, send to Queen Isyn to inquire. But I believe Nix."

"What? No! She's the imposter, not me." She clutched Cavan's arm. "Besides, I carry your child. I'm sure of it. I only waited to tell you the news—you cannot have me killed."

"My son." Wyn ceded the decision to him, raising his brows at Cavan's surprise. "This is a question of your queen. Your rule.

Thus, this is for you to decide, not me."

As king, he would no doubt face difficult decisions someday. This one was not. He turned to Natilde. "What would you have me do?"

Natilde gave Cavan a beseeching look, moistening her lips. "You see her. She's a frail thing. Not fit to be a queen. She's only a base servant, with nothing to offer the world. I'm your wife. You will find keeping me most *rewarding*. Execute her."

"Is that your sentence?" Cavan asked. Her face lit with hope—and conniving greed. He'd seen it in her all along and hadn't wanted to. "Execution for the one who dealt treachery instead of loyalty, cruelty instead of succor, brutal ambition over duty and responsibility."

"Yes." Natilde raised her chin and pointed at Nix. "She is all those things. A cruel, ambitious bully, who deserves a painful death."

"What say you, Princess Nix?" Cavan asked.

Nix looked on the woman with sorrow, her midnight gaze penetrating. "I cannot stomach more death. It would be best to imprison her. Search her things for information, send to my mother to warn her of whatever we may find, for I'm sure we shall. If she quickens in the interim, the babe will be blameless and of Cavan's blood. We would raise the babe accordingly."

"Spoken like a true queen." King Wyn nodded. "I concur with Prince Cavan's judgment and Princess Nix's solution. Let it be so."

"No!" Natilde screamed. "You can't do this. I'm a princess! Obey me!" Her wails dragged behind her as the guards took Natilde away.

King Wyn himself stepped down, took Nix's hand and led her up the steps to place her hand in his son's. "I fear we can never make things right for you."

She stood on tiptoe and kissed his cheek. "I will make things right. Nothingness is the origin of all things. Life will answer death."

Filled with pride and love, Cavan kissed her hand, and settled his bride beside him. The future lay before them, bright with promise.

EPILOGUE

Springtime
Years Later

GEESE SCATTERED, HONKING and flapping wings as the young prince and princess chased them around the pond. Nix laughed, rounding them up and herding the lot toward where Cavan awaited them. He took her hand, smiling at their son and daughter as they barreled up the path past them, then kissed her fingers, sending a trill of magical desire through her.

"You'll make gooseherds of our children yet," he commented, keeping her hand as they followed up the path to the road.

"I hope so. It's good for them to learn all aspects of the world and the kingdoms they'll someday govern. A wise man once told me that."

"Ha! A man who has done many foolish things."

She smiled up at his handsome face, his gray eyes gentle with love. "There's room for foolishness in the world, too. What news of Remus?"

He caught her up on the progress of the rebuilding efforts, bringing good news indeed. When they passed beneath the arched gate, they paused, as they always did. Sometime in that storm, the night they'd found each other, Falada's head had frozen in place, then cemented into stone. Her visage remained there always, ears high and eyes open, gazing with benediction upon all who passed beneath. Offerings of flowers lay scattered on either side, and people whispered that wishes made to her would be granted, as long as the prayer was offered from a heart empty of ambition and cruelty.

And if Falada—her spirit presence always near—sometimes whispered to Nix of certain things the King and Queen might do to ease the way for those wishes, none would be the wiser.

The Crown of the Queen

A Novella of the Twelve Kingdoms and the Uncharted Realms

by Jeffe Kennedy

It's been a lifetime since librarian Dafne Mailloux saw the coronation of the tyrant who destroyed her family. She did her part to pull him off the High Throne. But his daughter, the would-be Queen, and her sisters must still tame their conquest. If her victory is to last, Dafne must forge peace with the subtle, ruthless methods of a diplomat—and the worst memories of her life . . .

DEDICATION

To all the quiet bookworms, like me

~ **1** ~

"**D**AFNE, YOU'RE GOING to miss your own party."

I glanced up from the scroll I'd been copying to see Zynda standing on the other side of the table. From her wry smile and raised eyebrows, I gathered she'd been standing there for a while. The Tala—well, most people, but in particular the Tala—seemed quite bemused that I could be so blind and deaf to the world while immersed in words on the page. As a culture focused primarily on oral histories, the Tala weren't much for keeping documents at all. But a great deal of what they did have contained information I'd never seen anywhere else.

With a sense of opportunity running through my fingers as inevitably as a fistful of seawater, I'd spent my last days in Annfwn scanning for the rarest and most alluring documents—and then copying what I could, as fast as possible.

It wasn't that I didn't want to attend my going-away party—though I had never been much for the social whirl—it just marked the end of an idyll.

Time for me to go home. Or rather, back to Castle Ordnung, which was as close to a home as I'd ever had.

"There's so much here I haven't gone through," I answered, with a scowl for her amusement at my expense. "If it were anyone but Her Majesty summoning me, I'd find a way to delay."

Not only for the rare books, either. It would be difficult to leave this place, with the aquamarine water glittering beyond the library's white pillars, wound round with flowering vines. The brightly colored canvas overhead that reminded me of sails on ships—and served to keep off the worst of the rain—flapped with gentle mutters in the warm breeze off the water. A corner of the scroll I'd been copying lifted and I moved a smoothly polished seashell to weight it better.

"But you would never refuse Ursula." Zynda said it solemnly enough, but her deep blue eyes, radiant with Tala shapeshifter magic, gleamed with mischief. The Tala weren't much for authority, either.

"I don't wish to," I corrected her, meaning it despite my earlier gripe. I'd long cultivated the ambition of serving as councilor to the three daughters of the High King, in whatever capacity I could—with the lion's share of my ambition going toward the day the eldest, Ursula, ascended to the High Throne. Though I'd longed for High King Uorsin's downfall most of my life, that day had come sooner than even I had hoped for.

I hadn't wanted Ursula to have to kill her own father, however. Goddesses knew High King Uorsin had collected plenty of enemies over his miserable life. But not just anyone could have done what Ursula did—or paid the price I suspected she had. Regardless, the High Throne stood empty for Uorsin's Heir, and she'd called me on my promise of filling the role Derodotur had held for her father.

It wasn't in me to be superstitious, but word had also arrived of Derodotur's grim fate as one of the living dead. An image I couldn't shake, one far too close to how my future seemed when I awoke in the small hours of the night that were strangely so conducive to irrational feelings, like the creeping fear that by taking on his job, I might also fall to the same fate. Or I'd simply continue to live as I had since my family's castle fell to Uorsin—at most half-alive. I shook off the mood, giving Zynda a resolute smile. "I truly don't wish to refuse. I'll miss Annfwn, but there will be a great deal to do to ensure your cousin secures the High Throne."

Zynda brought the long fall of shining black hair over her shoulder, idly making a rope of it as she puzzled over that. "But she won, yes? The duel is over with. He's dead and the right to rule falls to her."

"It's not so simple in the Twelve as it is in Annfwn. I'm sure they crowned her immediately, but there are many legalities to see to, detractors and alliances to navigate. There will be many challengers to come, if they're not there already."

She shrugged that off as not her problem. Which it wouldn't be. The headaches would be entirely mine. *You wanted this*, I reminded myself. Ursula hadn't sent details—in fact, no written missive at all—only the message via her Hawks that an escort waited to bring me and the royal family's infant heirs to Ordnung.

"Well, I'm glad we're finally leaving tomorrow—it will be such an adventure!" Zynda smiled at my soft snort of disbelief. "At least for me. The lands of the Twelve Kingdoms must be so very different."

"You do know it will be autumn in Mohraya, yes? Being at the base of the mountains, they could get snow at any time. It may have snowed already."

"Frozen water," Zynda nearly sang the words, eyes sparkling with rapture as she gazed out at the gorgeous tropical sea she'd looked on all her life. "I can't quite imagine it. It must be so very beautiful."

"It's so very cold, is what it is."

She grinned at me undaunted and twisted up her rope of hair, securing the coil with a pair of long, jeweled hairpins she pulled from the pocket of her filmy dress. In many ways Zynda, a close cousin to the three princesses by way of their mother, Salena, looked most like Princess Andromeda—Andi, informally—with her dark hair and that sense of unsettling shapeshifter magic to her. But Zynda was built more like Ursula, tall and lean, in a softer way, without the warrior's muscles and scars. The barely-there Tala garb skimmed her slender frame in the same colors as the blossoms hanging so flagrantly from the vines around us.

"It will be lovely to be cool," she replied. "But I've packed all the things you said to." She began naming them off, displaying the enviable eidetic memory most of the Tala possessed. Nothing like training the mind to memorize oral histories from a young age to hone that ability. Then again, my old tutor at Castle Columba had always said there was no sense taking up memory storing something you could easily reference in a book.

"Is that everything?" Zynda looked so enthusiastic, so much the opposite of how I felt, that I had to laugh.

"It will have to be. Besides, the journey should take no more than three days, even with the babies, possibly less. I really appreciate your help with them."

"I like babies. Especially easy ones like Astar and Stella, who aren't shapeshifting yet."

"Glorianna help us if they do."

"You'll want to appeal to Moranu for help with that," Zynda corrected. "And it's when, not if."

"Stella has the mark, not Astar. Maybe he never will." Of

Salena's three daughters, only Andi had inherited the ability to shapeshift. Which was why she'd become Queen of the Tala, following in her mother's footsteps. Though it appeared that Queen Amelia, Astar and Stella's mother, had subtle magic of her own. Even Ursula, for all her hard-headed ways, the apparent epitome of the unchanging mossbacks, as the Tala called non-shifters, drew her fighting speed and flexibility from a touch of shapeshifter magic.

Zynda shrugged one golden-skinned shoulder. "Who knows what effect having Annfwn's magic spilling over all the Twelve will have? Astar may not need to be as pure-blooded to do it as he would have when the barrier still isolated Annfwn. Maybe the magic being everywhere will make it easier."

"Logically, as the magic disburses over a greater area, it should attenuate. Like water. Or air." Once the barrier had held magic inside Annfwn. Whatever Ursula had done when she killed Uorsin had also made the barrier disappear as if it never had been—or perhaps it had only moved. It would be interesting indeed to finally hear those details.

"Ah ah." Zynda shook a finger at me, trying to look like a stern teacher and failing terribly. "Magic isn't water or air. What if magic is more like fire and the more fuel it has, the hotter it burns?"

I frowned at her, then stretched, suddenly aware of the stiffness in my body from sitting so long on the stool. As the Tala rarely sat still, their chairs were never comfortable for extended periods. Zynda, true to her people, still stood, her bare feet whispering over the tiled floor in a perpetual dance to some internal song.

"Do you think that's the case?" I asked her. The implications of such a thing could be tremendous. I'd have to bring it to

Ursula's attention. Though what we'd do about it was another question.

Her face brightened in a teasing smile and she laughed. "I don't know. I only argued with you because you're so serious. Come, leave your scrolls. It's your last evening in Annfwn and we're having a party!"

She had a point about that. I would never make it through even a part of what I wanted to. Everything else was packed. Still, I hated to waste whatever time in the Tala library I could eke out. "Let me finish this one scroll, then I'll be down."

Zynda shimmied a happy dance, almost snakelike, which I thought was one of her forms—it seemed very likely, seeing her move that way. "The beach at sunset," she reminded me. "We'll have a bonfire, bake crabs in the coals, and dance. Everything is ready. If you're late, I'll send Zyr to drag you down."

"I'll be there," I promised her retreating back. I'd keep my word—I always did—but the sensation I'd missed something important nagged at me. Natural, with such a wealth of information and yet… I'd learned to rely on my intuition to find answers the answers I sought.

Not that I had a particular question. There was just so much I hadn't read over. Deciding one more copied scroll wouldn't make any difference, I left off the task and followed the impulse to open one of the chests in a row I'd never gotten to. I might not have an eidetic memory, but I could stuff a few more things into my head faster than I could copy. The contents of the first chest didn't dazzle me. Fascinating, yes, but nothing to satisfy the tickle that prodded at me. Same with the second chest.

The third, however—I knew as soon as I opened it. *Something special.* The parchment scrolls breathed antiquity, though they seemed remarkably better preserved than most everything else. I carried several to a nearby table and unrolled the first with a sense of reverence.

An entirely new language, similar to the written Tala language—related almost certainly—but far more sophisticated and complex. So much so that I couldn't hope to parse any of it in the scant time left. Setting aside the frustration that plagued me, I focused on the illustrations instead. Beautifully detailed, in vivid colors untouched by time. Fabulous, too. They showed islands dominated by perfect conical peaks, draped in jungle foliage.

And dragons flying through the sky.

In another, most improbable, a person with a quill and scroll sat next to a dragon of shining gold with its wings folded, both heads bent over the document as if they conferred. A long story beneath seemed to be what they discussed. Or created. Yet another showed a bleaker scene. Many dragons lay sleeping. No. They were dead, as people gathered around them, clearly mourning.

I studied them until it was too dark too see. Then, remembering my promise—and Zynda's threat to send her brother after me—I put them away again, tamping down my regret to fold in with all the others. My life had never been my own and I should be grateful to have a calling I believed in.

Gathering my things, I looked around the open-air library and said goodbye.

~ 2 ~

T HE SUN HAD long since lowered itself past the vast, flat horizon of the Onyx Ocean as I made my way down to the beach. My legs had grown stronger during my time in the cliff city, from trudging up and down the steeply winding curves of the roads and pathways. Younger and more athletic people than I took the many shortcuts—which included ropes, slides and various tunnels. I preferred to play it safe and take the long way. Besides, it let me take one last walk through the city. The "palace"—a glorified term for King Rayfe and Queen Andromeda's home, which also contained the library—perched near the top of the white cliff. Thus it took some time to wend all the way down to the beach.

I hadn't been in Annfwn long enough for the Tala to become accustomed to the sight of me. I didn't stand out nearly like Queen Amelia had, with her red-gold hair and extraordinary beauty, nor like Captain Harlan had, before they all left Annfwn to storm Ordnung. Of course, the Dasnarian mercenary stood out in any crowd, with his sheer muscled size. The Tala, though, were nearly uniformly dark-haired and golden-skinned, with eyes ranging through shades of blue and gray. So, my usually unremarkable brown hair and eyes, along with the light, freckled complexion that never quite tanned, continued to elicit interest from denizens of Annfwn.

It had been fun to be exotic, if only for a temporary excursion.

The Tala greeted me as I passed, no longer giving me that studied indifference they took on with other foreign visitors, and I replied reasonably well in their language. They constructed their phrasing very differently, using pitch to denote meaning as much as pronunciation, making it particularly difficult to master. Fortunately I would have Zynda to practice with in the future.

"There she is, our guest of honor and possessor of my lonely heart!" Zyr swept me into an impromptu dance, taking us in dizzying circles. "I was about to fly up and carry you down over my back."

I laughed, letting his infectious playfulness dispel my sense of foreboding. Unlike Zynda, he did not speak any of the Common Tongue of the Twelve Kingdoms and had been an enthusiastic—if overly flirtatious—tutor in helping me through my attempts at conversation in the liquid Tala language. I could never be sure how to process his wilder declarations. He delighted in teasing me, drawing me into riddles that turned out to be merely jokes.

"Don't go, Dafne," he crooned in my ear, stilling his mad circling. "Stay and be my lover. You can have all the scrolls you like. I'll even make you new ones."

Still laughing, I untangled myself from him. He'd been swimming, probably helping to catch supper, wearing only thin cotton pants, and he smelled of salt and warm skin. Like all Tala men, he wore his hair long, wildly unkempt, and he shared Zynda's deep blue eyes, though he stood much shorter and somewhat stockier.

"That's not how the scrolls work, Zyr!"

"Then teach me. Whatever it takes to win your heart."

"I have to go back to Ordnung. The High Queen needs me."

He clasped his hands over his bare chest and made a lovesick face. "I need you."

"The moment I'm gone, you'll find half a dozen pretty shapeshifter girls to distract you."

"Probably." Zyr flashed a grin. "But they won't be my serious mossback librarian." He used the Common Tongue word—had to, as the Tala had no parallel term—impressing me. "If you won't stay, then you must dance with me."

"We just did."

"More. So I can store them up, to take out and remember later."

"All right, then."

Evening fell soft and gentle over the beach. Moranu's moon, waxing toward full, rose from behind the high cliff, which glowed with candle and torch light from thousands of windows and open doorways. With no need to shield from inclement weather and practically no fear of physical attack, the Tala dwellings stood open to the night air. If the loss of the magic barrier began to affect the weather in Annfwn, the Tala would have many changes to make. For the time being, however, paradise persisted.

The fresh crab seemed to melt on my tongue and I became a little drunk as every person who embraced and kissed me farewell seemed to have a fresh goblet to press into my hand. Music flowed as freely as the ambrosial wine and I danced with Zyr until my feet were sore and only a few windows remained lit in the cliff city.

"I should go," I told him. "We'll be up early to ride out."

"Ah, don't say so." He pressed a kiss to my cheek, one of

hundreds my friends had showered upon me that evening, the Tala so easy with their affections.

"I must. Duty calls, not dancing."

"Well, perhaps these will last you until you can dance with another."

"I doubt there will be much of that in my future."

"That's a terrible thing to believe, pretty Dafne."

"I'll be advising Ursula in her role as High Queen, not drinking wine on the beach with handsome young shapeshifters."

He tossed back his hair, smiling his delight. "I knew you found me handsome! Come share my bed tonight. A good-bye present."

I was drunk enough to be amused instead of taken aback. Nothing like wine, dancing, and balmy nights to make the daunting sound possible. Vaguely tempting, but not enough to overcome long habit. "For me or for you?" I teased, putting him off.

Kissing my cheek again, lingering over it, he murmured in my ear. "For both of us. Something to share."

It would have been nice to be able to say yes, to be that woman. But I never had been, and if the pattern held true, I never would be.

"I'm afraid dances are all we can share, Zyr. But I'll always remember this night."

"Is there another, waiting for you back in your cold and harsh land? He will never know. It would be our secret. A special memory, just for us."

So very Tala with their morality as fluid as their language and record-keeping. "No, there isn't anyone. Never has been." More drunk than I thought, to have admitted that. Also, confiding in someone you'll never see again is somehow easier.

He sobered, a rare expression for him. "What holds you back?"

Not an easy question to answer. Goddesses knew I'd posed it to myself enough times. But I liked the way he'd asked it and I'd apparently had wine enough to give it a try. "I think I started out waiting for the right person, the right timing. I always expected the moment would arrive and everything would come together and I'd *know*. Then time kept passing and suddenly it seemed I'd waited too long. Somehow I missed my moment. And now I'm sort of… suspended, eternally waiting for this thing that won't ever happen."

Zyr listened intently, brows drawn in concentration. I'd likely butchered the language, going too fast and slurring the pitches in my long explanation. I offered a feeble laugh. "Sorry you asked?"

"No." He shook his head to confirm it. "Maybe you didn't miss the moment and you're simply waiting for it to arrive still."

I didn't think so, but I smiled at his relentless optimism. "Maybe so. But this isn't it."

"Only you can know, though I'm sorely disappointed not to be the one you've been waiting to find. Some people share themselves easily, like the bushes that produce clusters of berries, plenty for all to have and enjoy." He flashed a grin at that. "A few are like the *kalpa* tree, which bears a single fruit after many years, and is all the more precious for that. It can't be easy to wander the world searching for that other self."

Something about his words stuck in my heart and I gazed back, none of the words I sought coming to my tongue.

"I might not be the one, but we can share this much." He threaded long fingers into my hair, brushing it back from my temples and cupping my face. Rapt, I held still as he kissed me, tasting of wine and firelight, the warmth of the tranquil sea.

Lovely. Poignant.

And like a song not written for me.

I sighed against his mouth, in part for the sweetness of the kiss and in part for the disappointment that it didn't move me enough. With good humor, Zyr smiled and planted a final kiss on my forehead. "It's not me."

"I'm sorry."

"Don't be sorry, pretty librarian. I'll have my kiss with the *kalpa* tree to remember, the gift of the flavor of something rare."

"And dances." I reminded him, relieved that he didn't press and also seemed not to mind that I refused him.

"Yes. Good fortune in your wandering and seeking."

"There won't be much of that. Just the journey back to Ord-nung where I'll stay." Back to dwell over the bones of my family, for the rest of my days. The living dead.

"More waiting."

It sounded bad, put that way, over the background of my glum thoughts. "I'm sure I'll be far too busy to think about it much."

"Think about it," he advised. "Maybe you need to do less waiting and more wandering."

"I'll give it thought."

"Good." He pulled me into a few twirling steps. "Remember. No one can take away the dances you've already had."

His words gave me a shiver, the sense of an omen looming, much like that intuition from earlier. Given that Salena's blood sometimes came with the gift of prophecy, I tucked away his words, along with Zynda's. Knowledge is power, especially for one such as myself, whatever the source. It could come in useful someday.

$$\sim 3 \sim$$

W ITH STELLA STRAPPED in her knitted carry on my chest, I took in my last glimpse of the tranquil sea and firmly turned my back on it. My future lay ahead, up the road into the forests that shrouded the cliff city, over Odfell's Pass, and down into Castle Ordnung. Zynda carried Astar and their two Tala nurses accompanied us, along with four Hawks Ursula had sent into Annfwn to retrieve us.

There would be more to our escort at the bottom of the pass—probably a small army—to make sure nothing happened to the heirs to the High Throne. In truth, it would be a relief to hand the babies over. I'd been willing to stay with them in Annfwn while Ami, Andi, and Ursula went to deal with all that had befallen Ordnung, and I'd accepted the charge to serve as regent for the twins, should the unthinkable occur. Those responsibilities, however, were ones I did not covet, so hopefully it would never come to that.

I'd never wanted a throne—either the power of one or the power behind one.

Though the barrier around Annfwn had fallen, it wouldn't pay to advertise that fact, so Ursula would have kept the bulk of our escort outside the borders. Enough people longed for the bounty this mythical place offered to come here in hordes, with plunder on their minds. Accordingly, the Tala had increased their defensive efforts, both magical and physical. Thus, our small group passed quickly and easily over the pass, where a larger one would not.

Still, Ursula would no doubt be negotiating with King Rayfe to determine the delicate balance of easing Annfwn into being a kingdom with open borders. Even with Andi mediating between those two, the conversations would not be smooth. Probably one reason Ursula wanted me there with all haste. Accordingly, I spent time in the saddle reading up on a few histories I'd marked that told of similar alliances. Usually an empire conquered a kingdom—or a general like Uorsin conquered numerous kingdoms and forged them into one under his fist—but Rayfe would never agree to that and Ursula was not her father. We would need another model.

As we ascended into the mountains, the weather grew colder and we had to stop and put on heavier garments. One of the Tala nurses took Stella from me. I missed her warm weight, but not her attempts to grab the pages of my book with her sticky baby fingers. By the time we passed the lake where we'd camped that first night inside the barrier, the trees and flowers showed how fully autumn had encroached. Leaves that had remained tropically green for hundreds of years, if not more, displayed dazzling shades of ambers, golds, crimson and flame. As with everything in Annfwn, the colors seemed more intense—breathtakingly so—but it hurt my heart to see it.

When full winter arrived, would it slide down the mountains like a monster eating everything in its way? The lush fruits and blossoms, so long distanced from freezing temperatures, would wither and die, perhaps without recourse to revive when warm weather returned. I could only hope Rayfe and Andi had already thought of this and could perhaps prepare the Tala upon their return to Annfwn. I would remind them, though how much attention they'd pay me was another issue.

The perils of being an adviser only, with no real power.

Fortunately the weather remained clear and fine, with the Wild Lands at the bottom of the pass feeling more like late summer than fall. Those glorious hot-sun, sharply crisp days that come to the mountains only after the first frost. Remembering those went a long way toward reconciling me to rejoining the seasons. The small army I'd predicted to myself turned out to be quite large—and commanded by Captain Harlan himself, which I hadn't expected at all.

"Lady Mailloux." He greeted me with a bow when I dismounted, his Dasnarian accent adding a foreign flavor to my name. "It's good to see you again. How has your journey been thus far?"

"Uneventful." I surveyed the extensive forces arrayed around the valley; Ordnung guard and Harlan's Vervaldr mercenaries alike. "Should I expect otherwise from here out?"

"Perhaps not, but Her Majesty wants no accidents." He grimaced and I couldn't help but smile, imagining how much more strongly Ursula must have put it. "In light of that, if you're not too weary, I'd like to cover more distance today."

"We planned to ride all day, so that's fine." I stepped into the woods to answer the call of nature, then remounted. Harlan rode beside me, apparently being companionable, but it was clear he also personally guarded our little group, even as we were encircled by the soldiers all around. More than making sure of no accidents.

I pondered the possible significance of Harlan's presence. A good exercise for getting my head back into the morass of political subterfuge that was Ordnung, the nexus of every devious plot and great ambition in the Twelve. No more easy sunshine and days of study. Uorsin's demise would have solved one set of problems but, like the slain dragon's teeth sown in the soil of legend, armies would grow in their place—all hungry to claim power of their own.

Ursula might have sent Harlan because she trusted him the most. Which would mean they'd had no trouble over the information I'd discovered and relayed to her just before she left Annfwn. I'd found in a Dasnarian text that our mercenary captain also carried royal blood, as he was one of six younger brothers of Emperor Hestar and therefore in line for that throne, though at the bottom end. She'd forbidden me to warn him, however, and she was unlikely, given her hard-headed nature, to have brought it up in a rational discussion with him. It hadn't been difficult to predict how she'd react. Uorsin had trained her well to expect betrayal and more than one younger prince unlikely to gain his own throne had attempted to court her for a chance at hers.

Thus Harlan's being sent to escort me and the twins could also indicate a rift between him and Ursula. Ursula's Hawks, stubbornly closed-mouthed in their loyalty to her, had not said either way.

A delicate proposition to inquire, but I might not get another opportunity to ask him—and I absolutely needed to know which way this particular wind blew before I dealt with Her Majesty directly.

"So, all is well with you and the High Queen?" I asked, hoping the vague question would both sound politely general and entice him to confide. I liked Harlan. More, I appreciated his regard for Ursula and how well he saw through her prickly defenses and also managed to talk sense into her when no one else could. My job of advising her would be considerably easier with him keeping her balanced. I'd bitterly regretted telling her what I'd found out—especially the timing, with her riding out to a battle to reclaim Ordnung, a fight she needed Harlan and his Vervaldr to win—and had only done it because I felt sure she'd never forgive me if she found out that I'd known and hadn't said.

Harlan, a sharp observer and with intelligence as keen as his warrior's skills, slid me an amused glance. "You mean, after she tried to kill me for being a devious manipulator angling for the High Throne of the Twelve by seducing her?"

Oh Goddesses. As bad as I'd feared. But Ursula truly loved Harlan, I felt sure she did. I never predicted she'd go so far. "She didn't…" I managed to say through my horror and guilt.

To my shock, Harlan grinned in great good humor. "Well, she obviously didn't try very hard, as I'm still alive. But she drew blood before she settled into shutting me out and ordering me from the Twelve."

Worse and worse. "Oh no. Captain Harlan—I'm so very sorry."

"Ah." He nodded to himself. "I should have realized you were the one to find my name in the books and tell her."

"Yes. I shouldn't have told her. I should have kept it to myself."

"Eh." He lifted one big shoulder and let it fall. "I would have told her, if it had once occurred to me. If I had, she wouldn't have taken it as such a betrayal. The mistake was mine—a foolish oversight that caused unnecessary pain." He sighed heavily, as if deeply despondent.

Oh no. "Then…she's sent you away? You are no longer—"

He burst out in his booming laugh. "I shouldn't tease you so, Lady Mailloux. Ursula and I are fine. She forgave me, once I cornered her and forced her to talk to me. It turned out for the good because the altercation made her face how unreasonable her reaction was—and how she must guard against falling into her father's paranoid ways.

"No—I am here because she trusted me to see you and babies safely home. I have no loyalty to Dasnaria, my brothers, or acquiring power for them. I care not whether I see any of them ever again. Ursula is the one I love, the center of my world. She is everything."

Extraordinary how he admitted his feelings so easily. Such a hard-looking man, muscle-bound and poised to fight, sharp eyes scanning the countryside for signs of trouble even as he laughed loudly and spoke softly of love. He and Ursula deserved each other, in the best possible sense. With her heroic courage and terrifying sense of responsibility, no one less than a man like Harlan, with his complete and utter devotion, would possibly work for her.

Tamping down a surge of unattractive envy—after all, I would not trade places with Ursula for the world, as I had never possessed the skills or calling to be queen—I catalogued my questions. Best to discover as much as I could before entering the castle.

"Has she made you her official consort then?" We'd have problems either way if she had or if she hadn't.

He snorted. "No. It matters little to me, but apparently she can't until after she's officially crowned High Queen."

Appalled, I gaped at him. "There's been no coronation yet? Why ever not? That should have happened first thing following Uorsin's death. I'm surprised Lady Zevondeth, at least, has not raised a fuss on the protocol of that." I'd just assumed she was already High Queen. This was bad news, indeed.

Shaking his head in sorrow, he said, "Alas, that aged worthy survived Uorsin by only two days. She died in her bed and received a fine funeral, despite everything."

"I'm sorry to hear it," I murmured, wishing her safely to Glorianna's arms. Typical of the stubborn old lady, to have survived Illyria's rampages and take death in her own way. I turned my mind back to the business of the living. "They'll start whispering that Ursula is a pretender to the throne."

"They already are. That started up almost immediately—and not in whispers. Some are quite loud in their objections."

"Of course." I wanted to bang my forehead on the book I carried, but it might startle my horse. "What is she waiting for?"

"She says she's too busy." He phrased it neutrally, but gave me a wry glance, waiting for my reaction.

Which was to groan and roll my eyes. Banging my head on the book might be a good idea after all. "She's *too busy*. Can't you sic Andi and Ami on her?"

He shook his head. "They've tried talking to her. She won't even discuss it."

Uh-oh. Not a good sign at all. "Does she not want the throne now, after all that's happened?" I asked it carefully, making sure no one could overhear.

"It's not that. You know her as well as anyone. She could never *not* take the throne. The responsibility for the Twelve is the fabric of her being. They could ship her overseas and she'd keep trying to do her job."

All true. "Then what do you think is stopping her?"

"My Essla is…" He frowned. Reconsidered. "She's suffering considerable guilt over killing her father. I suspect she's resisting because she feels she doesn't deserve the throne. When she recovered from…whatever it was those three did, practically the first words out of her mouth upon regaining consciousness was a demand for her own execution."

~ 4 ~

I CLOSED MY eyes against that image—and against the plaguing sense that I should have been there. Of course she had felt that way. "Wait. Back up. Regaining consciousness—what happened?"

Harlan squinted up at the brilliant blue that only autumn seems to bring to the sky. "I don't know that I can explain and I stood as close as anyone. You heard that when we retook Ordnung, Ursula killed Illyria?"

"Yes." That much news had filtered over the pass. "Is it true your Mistress of Deyrr converted half the population of the castle and township into the walking dead?"

"She may have been Dasnarian, but she was never mine." He went on before I could apologize for misspeaking. "We don't have good numbers as yet. It seems she used recruits and others brought in from impoundment gangs. But yes, we have burned a great many."

I must have made a face, imagining that, because he gave me a sympathetic glance. "I agree. All that gives them true death is dismemberment, then burning. You've escaped seeing the worst of it. Count yourself lucky."

I did, though the unsettling thought pricked at me that these undead might only appear to have found true death because ashes cannot move. What if their spirits remained trapped in some way? I didn't quite believe in the rose-covered bower of Glorianna's arms that some saw as what awaited them, returning to the mother's love beyond death. I'd told Ami once after she buried her husband, the good and noble Prince Hugh that I believed we move on to other lives, much as ashes become soil that grows into trees again. I hadn't been mouthing comforting platitudes—I truly believed that.

Ashes kept somehow eternally suspended between life and death could never do that.

"Ursula did not dispatch Illyria entirely on her own," Harlan was saying. "Queen Andromeda used magic against the priestess while King Rayfe brought his shapeshifters in by breaking the Rose Window."

"Oh no, not again."

"Yes." Harlan chuckled. "Rayfe seemed most pleased with himself."

"I can just imagine. What kind of magic did Andi use?"

"Some sort of blue lightning."

Why had I even asked?

Harlan acknowledged the unhelpfulness of his answer with a fatalistic shrug. "Then Queen Amelia called on Glorianna to dissolve the protective barrier Illyria had placed around herself—one much like the Annfwn barrier."

"Interesting."

"Yes. I tell you this because it has bearing on the final confrontation. Uorsin emerged from his rooms where he'd been barricaded."

I'd heard that part, but groaned in frustration at his cowardice regardless.

"I agree. Ursula took the cabochon topaz from her sword,

which is truly a perfect sphere that her mother gave her, called the Star of Annfwn."

"She did know where it was all along."

"Indeed. She swallowed it and—"

"Swallowed it, as in down her throat?"

"To her stomach where it has apparently remained. After coating it with her blood and that of her sisters." He nodded at my incredulous look. "I witnessed it myself. She then fought Uorsin, challenging him to abdicate. The Star somehow allowed her to channel Salena's magic."

"Salena, who is dead." As in eighteen years dead, not freshly undead. What a world we'd entered, that we'd have to specify the difference.

"The very one. I told you it's not easily explained. The Star also… aligned the three sisters, is the only way I can describe it. They invoked their goddesses and when Ursula ran Uorsin through with her sword, the moment his blood hit the earth, it was as if I stood inside an enormous temple bell that had been struck."

"Whoa."

"Yes." His voice held the softness of wonder at it, then he gave me a wry glance. "I am a practical man, but something … huge happened."

"The barrier fell."

"That and it felt like…something released. A great wave of magic crashing through a cracked dam. All three sisters collapsed. Rayfe, Ash, and I all feared at first they'd died."

"They were there, too?"

"Yes. Amelia and Andromeda awoke within the hour. Ursula…not for some time and only after Ash used his healing powers on her."

"So you were all a part of it—this spell, or what have you—and Ursula the focus."

"That seems to be the case. Amelia says that the land accepted the sacrifice and Andromeda says that something called the Heart of Annfwn is connected to the Star in Ursula. That's privileged information, by the way."

I arched a brow at him, surprised. "If it's privileged, am I meant to know it?"

"Yes. Ursula told me to make sure you knew everything you need to." He gave me a canny smile. "As we all know you do regardless, whether you admit to it or not."

"I understand now why the news was chary of details," I finally said, thoughts whirling as I assembled it all. "Though it makes more sense if Ursula has been reluctant to take the crown."

"Among other things," Harlan agreed. "Uorsin also admitted to murdering Salena. Bragged of it, in truth. That went hard on all of them." He studied my face. "But you are not surprised."

No, I wasn't. Though I'd never wanted to say as much. Especially for someone in my tenuous position in the royal household—not exactly a prisoner of war, not officially a ward of the Crown—survival depended on tact and political acumen. Which did not mean sharing my suspicions that the High King had deliberately murdered his queen. "I liked Salena. She was kind to me when she didn't need to be. We'd both lost our families and I think… we recognized that in each other."

"How old were you when Castle Columba fell?"

"Six. Nearly seven. I don't remember very much except the awfulness of the siege, how afraid and angry everyone was. Boredom and moments of stark terror. Being hungry." Other, darker things that I didn't care to examine.

"Difficult, especially for a small child. Not understanding fully, knowing only that the adults, the bedrock of your world, were coming apart."

Oh yes. The weeping and the shouts. People disappearing, never to return. The wounded, screaming in the night, and the silence after somehow worse.

"You were the only survivor?"

"Of my family, yes. The story is that a healer dug me out of a hidey-hole buried under rubble. Four days after the siege ended."

"Ah." His face creased with sorrow. "How terrible that must have been."

"It rained, so they think I lived on the rainwater that leaked through a crack. I don't remember it." Except in sharp-edged fragments here and there. I shook it off. "I begin to see how you manage Ursula so well. You draw confessions out of people."

"It's better, so teaches the tradition I follow, for warriors to air the old traumas. Open the wounds to let them heal."

"I am no warrior." The thought made me smile at the absurdity. "Only a librarian."

"We are all warriors in our own lives—fighting the battle to become who we most long to be."

I let that go, though it sounded like an overly grand way to view my small existence. "I think of my experiences more as formative. They shaped me, but are long scabbed over. As for Salena's death, I was a teenager then. They put about that she died of childbirth sickness, but . . . she wasn't ill. Not that way. So no, I'm not surprised. But I can see that Ursula, in particular, would have taken that news hard. She wanted to believe her father better than that."

"In many ways, she still struggles with that old faith she had in him."

"He had a deep hold on her, but it's good she has you to help her with it."

"And you. We were all relieved that she sent us to retrieve you. She will heed your good counsel."

I nearly snorted at *him* this time, relieved to be on the firmer ground of managing a mercurial ruler. "Her Highness does not listen to my advice all the time. Not even most of the time."

"She will. You will simply have to make the case to her for the coronation to happen immediately. We will all back you."

"You've discussed it amongst yourselves?"

He narrowed his eyes, face going neutral. "I will deny it if you say so."

I laughed; half amused, half frustrated. "So you're all just throwing me at the dragon to save yourselves."

"We will help you. Out of range of her fiery breath," he added with a grin, then sobered. "The situation is tense, Lady Mailloux. Magic has gone wild, causing pandemonium everywhere. The more aggressive of the Twelve pursue cases of patricide and treachery against Ursula. They whisper for her execution, call her right to rule into question at court, and she cannot bring herself to deny their claims, overtly or to herself."

"Hypocrites. Them, not her," I hastily added.

"Indeed. Queen Andromeda is feeling the strain of the barrier, which seems to pull at her still, though in a way she can't explain. Rayfe anticipates that Annfwn will be pillaged, fears for his wife, and wishes to return home as soon as possible."

"But Andi won't leave Ursula with the situation so unstable."

"And Amelia won't leave her either, nor go to Windroven without the babies, although there are disturbing reports of strange phenomena in that region."

"Such as?"

"I'll let you hear them for yourself, lest I color your perceptions with a misunderstanding of your Common Tongue." A sly deflection on his part. He understood our language better than some native speakers. But I had no grounds to press him to share what he did not wish to. "Never fear, Lady Mailloux." Harlan grinned at me in his genial way. "We shall not grow bored any time soon."

~ 5 ~

T HE FIRST THING that hit me as we rode up to the great
gates of Castle Ordnung was the absence of the pennants
that had always, *always* flown from the towers, since the first and
tallest had been raised.

I hadn't expected to feel the lack, to have any sense of nos-
talgia for the missing banners. But even before he'd finished
razing Castle Columba and building Ordnung on its bones,
Uorsin's flag had hung over the camp where we'd all lived after
Columba fell and the Great War ended. I didn't remember
everything about those days, but some memories persisted with
an almost fever-dream intensity to them. The armies, tearing
down the ruins of my family home, using ropes and teams of
men to pull down the few walls that remained, while others beat
on stone with hammers and other tools. The air had been gray
with dust and stank of burning bodies.

Then the first shining white tower had grown like a stem
sprouting from the soil, shooting up, then blossoming with
Uorsin's bear running against the sky, alive and ravenous. For a
while, I'd dreamed of that bear every night. Crimson as fresh
blood, it chased and caught me, no matter where I ran. Through
forests, through the tent camp, through battlefields littered with
the dead, through the halls of Columba, though I knew they no

longer existed.

Once I'd awakened to Queen Salena's hand on my brow. A blue light spun in her palm making her eyes glow with silver. She hadn't spoken, only smiled and stroked my forehead. I'd fallen asleep with a sense of cool sweetness that calmed and sated me. Always after, when she spoke of the loveliness of Annfwn, I'd imagined that feeling came from there. That had been one reason I'd determined to convince Ursula to let me go there, much as she tried to prevent me, to keep me safe. A piece of my younger self had demanded to know, a far stronger pull than safe practicality. Rare for me.

Once Ordnung had been finished, banners for all the Twelve joined their conqueror's, flying from the many towers, the bear topping them all. To my bemusement, they had gone from being a sign of defeat to a symbol of continuity, that my life had not shattered again.

The emptiness of the towers hit me with that old dizzying sense of loss, and I groped through it to find words to ask Harlan about it. "You took down *all* the pennants?"

Harlan frowned, following my gaze. "Illyria must have. They weren't flying when we took the castle." He seemed to search his memory. "I'm sure they weren't. And you're the first to mention the lack."

"I imagine it didn't feel like the highest priority, but as with the coronation, these things must be addressed. The key to an even transfer of regimes is making it seem as if nothing has really changed."

"Except for the tyrannical abuse of power."

Well, yes. "For external presentation, to prevent anyone from thinking to take advantage, there can be no apparent cracks. It must seem as if Ursula is simply continuing what Uorsin started."

"You can explain that to Her Majesty. I look forward to it, in fact."

I glared at him and he grinned down at Astar, riding wide-eyed in his carry, strapped to Harlan's broad chest. "Lady Mailloux has a fierce mien," he said to the baby prince, "but never fear. She is a softie inside. Just don't get fingerprints on her books or not even your mother will be able to protect you."

As if on cue, Amelia, looking more like a girl dressed to dance at a Feast of Glorianna than a queen, squeezed impatiently through the opening gates. Her red-gold curls shimmered and the intense violet blue of her eyes shone through her tears. "Oh, thank Glorianna!" she cried in her musical voice as she ran up to Harlan's stirrup, jumping up and down with her arms out-stretched for Astar. "Give me my baby. Where is Stella?"

"Let the man get off his horse, brat." Ash followed behind her, his scarred mouth twisted by a wide, pleased smile. "And if you took a moment to look, you'd see your cousin Zynda has Stella. How you could miss the head of hair on that child I don't know."

"Or the shrieking," I added.

As soon as Stella, whose black curls indeed sprang wildly round her head, heard her mother's voice, she'd started fussing and now ramped up to a full-throated wail that demanded instant satisfaction.

"Sounds just like her mother," Ash commented in his raspy, damaged voice, as Zynda, with her liquid Tala grace, uncoiled from the saddle, leapt down, and handed him the indignant princess. Harlan had already lowered a much-calmer Astar to his mother's impatient arms, so Ash held out Stella close enough for Ami to rain kisses and coos on her also. Already the twins had grown enough to make it unwieldy to hold both at once. Ash surveyed me with his bright green gaze, so clear and cool in his craggy face. "Good to see you again, Lady Mailloux. We've need of your level head and extensive learning."

"So I've been told." I flicked a glance at Harlan, who'd dismounted and held up a hand to help me down, his expression studiously bland.

Neither did Ash take the bait. "Any trouble?" he asked Harlan.

"More on the way there. A few skirmishes on the way back." Harlan took note of my surprise. "Our advance teams handled them. I didn't mention to you as I didn't want you to worry."

"I'm perfectly fine with not worrying," I assured him. Another reason I could never trade places with Ursula—or Andi or Ami, even—as I didn't have a bold or heroic bone in my body. Give me a quiet room full of books over adventure every time. Maybe seeing the pennants gone and remembering those early days of Uorsin's triumph, the old memories of Salena and the nightmares, had left a chill over me, but I wanted nothing more at that moment than to find a safe cubby and curl up in it.

Not unlike my six-year-old self, first hiding, then trapped for days in the darkness of that hole while my family, all my people, burned and died. Harlan and his interest in airing old traumas had done nothing more than dig up things best left lying quiet.

He and Ash were discussing the various groups that had attacked—or needed to be chased off—and I made myself focus on that instead.

"The organized group of 'merchants' headed for Annfwn sounds like the greatest concern," Ash mused.

"Yes," Harlan replied, gesturing us through the gates. "Though that particular set won't be bothering anyone again, we can certainly expect more of the same. Honestly, that strange monster my patrol put down concerns me most."

"You're not accustomed to the Wild Lands yet," Ash argued. "And your men are not schooled in the creatures there. It could have been something ordinary with—"

"With four legs, a pair of wings, and claws as big as a man's head?" Harlan interrupted, then shrugged with an easy grin. "And we may as well table this discussion until we all sit down together, as the High Queen and King Rayfe will simply make us go over it all in detail again."

"She's not the High Queen," I said, feeling I needed to. Might as well practice before facing the dragon herself. They all stared at me with varying expressions of consternation and shock.

Anger, on Ami's part. "Who else would you have?" she demanded.

"Nobody else, Queen Amelia." I kept my tone mild. "The point is that she isn't High Queen until she's crowned. Nor is she Her Majesty. By calling her that, you're all letting her get away with ducking what she needs to do. There are reasons for these protocols, not the least of which are legal ones. With no one officially sitting on the High Throne, there *is* no Twelve Kingdoms—only thirteen kingdoms ready to go their own ways again. I'm astounded none of the kings and queens have cited this as grounds to secede. There's historical precedent for this. We'd have to go to war, conquer them all over again to get them back. I, of all people, am no lover of Uorsin's methods, but he *did* create peace. It's irresponsible of Ursula to risk setting us back this way."

Ash shook his head, laughing in his rough, voiceless way. "Do you promise to repeat that speech to Ursula where I can listen?"

"I prefer to be out of striking distance, myself," Harlan said, implacable, but his eyes gleamed with amusement.

Ami sighed. "Dafne is right, but . . . there's a lot you don't know. Go a little easy on her," she said to all of us.

Ash rubbed a hand up her back. "We all have our roles. You support her and Dafne can lay down the law. That's why we need her here. Ursula will listen to her."

I only hoped he was correct about that.

~ 6 ~

U RSULA WAS HOLDING court in the great hall. She wasn't seated on Uorsin's throne or her own, but stood before them—wearing fighting leathers and her sword.

The hole where Glorianna's rose window had been gaped empty still, autumn air and sunshine filtering in. Always lean, Ursula now looked nearly gaunt, with shadows under her eyes. Queen Andromeda sat in her traditional throne as Princess of the Realm, but with King Rayfe beside her in the one that had always been Ami's. Though I'd become accustomed to the Tala's appearance, Andi and Rayfe with their loose dark hair streaming over the shoulders of their colorful silks, the crackle of magic about them, seemed wild and exotic in the harsher frame of Ordnung.

Ursula nodded somberly at the petitioner who spoke to her, then fastened her sharp gaze on us over his shoulder. She surveyed us all thoroughly, and seeing that none of us bore injuries, something relaxed in her face.

"Has she sat on the High Throne yet?" I asked Harlan as softly as I could.

"Refuses," he murmured back.

I sighed mentally. We had a great deal to do.

Ursula finished with the petitioner, a man I didn't recognize—more catching up for me to do, with so many who'd populated the court gone and new ambassadors coming in—held up a hand to the others waiting and beckoned us forward. She kissed Astar and Stella on their foreheads, raised her chin and her voice, announcing, "I welcome back to Ordnung Queen Amelia of Avonlidgh and her son and daughter, who I declare to be my heirs to the High Throne, Prince Astar and Princess Stella."

That sent an ascending murmur of astonishment through the assembly, as the existence of Stella had been a secret until now. For myself, I clamped my mouth shut over the protest that she, first, couldn't name anyone heir, since she wasn't yet the High Queen, and second, that she couldn't declare two heirs at once, especially one that didn't officially exist as, third, Stella had yet to be named and entered into the records as Amelia's daughter.

Ursula, never anything less than observant, caught my expression anyway, a line forming between her brows. "Welcome back, Lady Mailloux. You were missed." At least she'd gotten the warning about making more declarations.

"Your Highness." I curtsied, careful to observe protocol.

She narrowed her eyes at me, then greeted the rest of the Tala delegation, seeming especially pleased to see her cousin. With Harlan, she simply brushed his forearm with the tips of her fingers, but the look she gave him said everything—and went a long way toward easing my guilt over causing disharmony between them.

In light of our arrival, she adjourned court for the day, a move that sent another wave of reaction through the room, this time of disgruntlement. In future days, I would assume Derodotur's duties—assembling, reviewing, and prioritizing petitions—and attempt to keep a reasonable timetable for Ursula's decisions. Uorsin, especially in the last few years, had grown increasingly unpredictable and often canceled court on a whim, or didn't show when expected.

If I had my way, we'd establish an orderly schedule that would allow for issues to be addressed, leave some room for unexpected crises, and give Ursula time and space to retain her humanity.

Perhaps to first regain it.

"I'll have food sent to my rooms," she said after the courtiers dispersed. "We can meet there and—what, librarian? Enough with the baleful gazes."

Ah well, might as well start off as I meant to go on. "Your Highness, perhaps a more formal location?"

The scars high on her cheekbone whitened and her hand fell to the hilt of her sword. The end, where the cabochon topaz had been, was twisted with rough edges. Another broken thing. "I'm not using *his* study."

"There are alternatives to the former High King's study. The family's private dining hall would make fine council chambers."

She gave me long stare, took in the expressions of the others. Nodded. "Fine. I'll ask Lise to—"

"Allow me, Your Highness." Before she could stop me, I found a serving girl to notify the chatelaine of our plans and to see that the room I'd suggested be quickly readied. And to send me writing materials along with food. Coming back, I found the three couples in deep conversation, discussing the vandals and beasts Harlan and his troops had encountered on the journey to and from Annfwn, including the one he'd described to Ash.

"I've never heard of such a creature." Ursula sounded dubious, frowning at Harlan.

"You saw odder ones in Annfwn," he replied.

"Not ones like that." Rayfe looked equally perplexed. "I wouldn't know what to call it, even in my language."

"A gryphon," I supplied. "At least as how they're described in the old tales."

"How old do you mean?" Ursula wanted to know, brow furrowed.

"Old enough not to be able to date them accurately. Certainly before Annfwn sealed itself off."

Ami nodded slowly. "I remember some of those. When Dafne and I studied the ancients and their wild magic." During that long, snowy spring at Windroven, while she'd been pregnant.

"It puts some of the other rumors we've been hearing in a new perspective," Ursula mused. "I've sent some of the Hawks' scouts to clarify reports and get accurate information, but even more eyes and ears might help. I don't like sitting here, blind and deaf. Maybe Jepp?"

Ash gave a slight shake of his head. "I've healed her as much as I can, but even with the barrier down and magic flowing out, it's not the same for me as being *in* Annfwn. Plus it feels like the magic is . . . eddying in some ways. I couldn't do as much for her as I did for Harlan inside Annfwn for example, and Jepp's wound was equally mortal."

"Jepp was mortally wounded?" I asked. I hadn't heard that.

As no one else seemed inclined to speak up, Ash replied. "Uorsin nearly gutted her, but she'll be all right. It took a great deal out of her and she needs to recover. She's restless, yes, but better for her to stay close another day or two."

I sighed. I liked Jepp, the boisterous and flirtatious woman who served as Ursula's best scout. I'd have to go find her later. "Information is good, but we have important decisions to make on matters directly before us. Matters of protocol and precedents."

Ursula grimaced, but banished her reluctance with a brisk nod. "I suppose that's why I recalled you. Let's get this over with, then."

Ami and Ash went to settle the babies in the nursery, planning to meet us in the council chambers. Andi embraced me with a smile and with her back turned to Ursula, rolled her eyes. "Good to have you with us, Dafne." She took Rayfe's proffered arm and they strolled ahead of us. I walked with Ursula and Harlan flanking me, feeling very like a small cat trapped between two wolves twice my size.

"Are you managing me, librarian?" Ursula asked mildly. A tone that didn't fool me for a moment.

"Somebody needs to," Harlan commented in the same tone.

"Don't start with me." She shot him a glare over my head. "Just when I was feeling all sentimental over missing you."

He grinned at her. "I love you, too, my fierce hawk."

They made me laugh. This was home, something I'd forgotten in my time away. "I'm happy to leave you to your devices, Your Highness, if you don't wish me to advise you. I'm sure the library needs extensive work."

She huffed. "Every thrice-damned thing in Ordnung needs work. It's like a battlefield after the armies have destroyed every last living thing and soaked the soil with blood."

As it had been after Columba fell. Though it wouldn't occur to Ursula that she evoked that image for me. It did to Harlan, however, and he set a heavy hand on my shoulder for a moment. There and gone. We stepped into the old family dining hall, which had fallen into disuse over the years—and then clearly pressed into recent service as sleeping chambers for many people at once during the crisis, when Ordnung had been packed tight with a population forbidden by Uorsin to leave. Servants were working to get up the worst of the detritus, but restoring the room to full functionality would take some doing.

How many of the people who'd made those blanket pallets on the floor had been turned into creatures of Deyrr and then burned?

Ursula surveyed the room with aggravation and disgust. "Still think this is a good idea?"

Her words were deliberately cutting, but under it lay a grief that haunted her eyes. No wonder they all danced around her. And yet that wasn't what she needed. I'd known Ursula all her life, since Salena handed the indignant baby to me and told me I held the future High Queen. Ursula would cripple herself trying to take responsibility for the past, if we let her. Time to focus on the present and future.

As the servants had done what they could without hours more work—the open windows helping to freshen the room considerably—I sent them on their way and chose a seat. Andi, eyes stormy with concern, sat also while Rayfe restlessly prowled the room, examining the portraits that hung on the walls. All of Uorsin in various poses and life stages, his presence heavy both on and in the walls. Perhaps we should follow his example and tear down the castle, build another on its undead ashes.

Goddesses, I was in a morbid mood.

Ursula seemed poised to follow Rayfe's example, but Harlan moved to the head of the table, holding the chair for her with steady, implacable courtesy. She capitulated, rolling her head on her neck and then folding her hands on the scarred table. Harlan took up position behind her, ever standing guard.

"I appreciate you answering my summons, Dafne. Though if

you wish to return to Annfwn, I understand. I know you loved it there."

"Thank you, Your Highness, but I'm here to stay, as long as you'll have me."

"It's only us. You can dispense with the formalities."

"All right then, along those lines, I need permission to speak frankly to you."

Her gray eyes went steely. "I've told you before that I value your advice and wouldn't censure you for your words."

"Good. I already said this to Ash and Ami, so I'll start there. Nobody should address you as High Queen or Your Majesty."

It would have been funny, the astonishment on her face and Andi's. Rayfe tossed me a look full of wicked amusement, shook his long hair back and leaned on the wall next to the open window, to all appearances like a man preparing to enjoy a spectacle. The wounded pain under Ursula's quick return to composure stopped my own smile.

"You believe I should step aside for another then." She nodded, confirming something to herself. "Face the rule of the law as a murderer."

~ 7 ~

I MANAGED NOT to scowl at her and lobbed the argument back in her lap. "Let me ask you this—who killed King Erich?"

She frowned, suspicious of my direction. "He fell in the conflict, but—"

"Will you be seeking his murderer to bring to justice?"

Sighing out an impatient breath, she tapped her fingers on the table, her nails ragged, with soil beneath. "I see where you're going with this, but killing a man in battle is not the same thing as assassinating the High King in cold blood."

"Why not?"

"Librarian, we don't need to engage in a philosophical discussion."

"Indulge me. Explain to me how these are not the same sort of battle, simply on a different scale."

She scowled, gray eyes dark with troubling thoughts, and it seemed everyone in the room held their breath, waiting for her answer. Staying clear of the dragon's breath. At last she unbent and inclined her chin. "All right. I cannot. Then why shouldn't I be High Queen, according to your logic?"

"I never said that. You should be and will be. We need you on the High Throne—following an ostentatious coronation ceremony, sanctioned by the Temple, attended by as many witnesses as possible, as soon as we can arrange it."

She brushed that aside. "That. I don't have time to—"

"Let me lay it out for you." I interrupted again before she could dig in on this with me also. In more detail than I had before, I explained the legalities and historical precedents. Ami and Ash arrived as I spoke. She seated herself quietly and Ash took position at her shoulder, leaving the four of us at the table. I understood their being careful of their relative rank and position in the conversation—though Rayfe arguably belonged at the table and simply preferred to prowl—but I didn't exactly belong there either. Still, I needed the surface to make notes as I spoke. I broke off only when servants returned with food and wine, which no one appeared ready to touch, taking up my case again when they left. No sense spreading word of our tenuous position faster than it would speed anyway.

"So," I wound up. "This is what I suggest be our order of priorities. One, get the pennants flying again, which means we need one for you as I'm assuming you don't want to use your father's."

"But can I, if I'm not High Queen?" Ursula said it with some acerbity, not pleased, but at least convinced of my points and focusing on the issues. Better.

"Yes. We have precedent there. Uorsin did it before his coronation."

"You remember that?" Andi asked with interest.

"I do, and I think we should replicate what he did as closely as possible." I held up a hand to forestall the biting remark Ursula had nocked to fire at me. "Only as regards ceremony and precedent. I'll get to that. Second, we need to polish up Ordnung. Fix the rose window, plant flowers, get every room cleaned. Create the illusion of prosperity."

"People are starving out there, librarian," Ursula broke in. "Some places in chaos. Magic setting off strange changes, on top of our already long-term crises of drought and starvation. Now we have this gryphon and rumors of river monsters and volcanoes rumbling. Not to mention Stefan calling for my head."

"Which is why you need to present yourself and your rule as competent and flourishing. *You* are the savior of Ordnung and the Twelve. You're our hero. You need to step up and be that, even if you don't feel it."

"I *don't* feel it," she snapped. Harlan touched her shoulder and she surprised me by leaning into his hand, closing her eyes briefly. Then opened them and fixed me with her hawkish stare. "But I see your point. Continue."

She reminded me of Uorsin and Salena both as I navigated my way through explaining the rest of my plan. Sometimes by a flicker of her expression, she hinted that she recognized I used her own tactics against her, handling her as I'd so often observed her deft management of the former High King.

I finished summarizing—bring in people from the township if necessary, but get Ordnung in shape for the ceremonies. Stella needed to be acknowledged and named and it wouldn't hurt to formally repeat it for Astar, as well. Coronation, with renewed treaties and vows of loyalty. Naming of *one* heir.

"You've been thinking about this a great deal," Ursula finally said, with a slight smile. She had relaxed. Everyone had.

"I had a lot of time to read," I answered.

"The window should not be Glorianna's alone," Ami spoke up for the first time since she'd come in. "Nor should the blessing at the Coronation. If you're starting a new era, everything you do should reflect all three goddesses equally."

"Why not?" Ursula returned with a wry grimace. "They got us into this mess, according to you. Fine. We'll commission a new window today, as that will take some time for the glaziers to make, much as it grates on me to spend resources on something only for show. This window," she pointed a long finger at Rayfe, who grinned lazily back, "you will not break. Ami, would you design it?"

"I'd be happy to." She looked delighted, in fact. Perhaps the magic that made her inhumanly beautiful infused her talents also, because Ami had a decided gift for creating beauty. "And for your personal banner, a hawk. With a rabbit in its talons," she added, mischief glinting in her twilight eyes.

Ursula snorted and shook her head, but Harlan—whose name meant "rabbit" in Dasnarian—smiled in placid appreciation for the joke.

While the more lighthearted mood persisted, I went in for the part she really wouldn't like. We'd been down *this* road before and it had turned out badly. "Also, if you're to be High Queen, you need to dress the part."

As I'd predicted to myself, she darkened. We both remembered too well how Uorsin had reacted when she wore her mother's jewels. But that had been the fault of his unstable character, not the plan itself. Never mind that it had been my plan and turned out disastrously. I still believed in it. And in her.

"No more fighting leathers in formal court," I persisted before she could cut off the conversation. "In fact, until you're crowned, you should only hold informal court. You don't need to wear gowns, but you should look like the High Queen, if only then. For the actual coronation though, you should have a gown, an elaborate one that represents who you are as a ruler. One that we can have you painted in, for your formal portrait."

She visibly cringed—not out of irritation, either—and Harlan stroked a hand over the back of her neck, giving me a warning look. Something about the coronation gown struck a nerve. I didn't know what, but Harlan did. "She doesn't have to, not if—"

"I can handle a silly thing like a dress," Ursula interrupted, brushing the tension from the air like encroaching cobwebs. "I'll give it thought and decide on something. What else?"

"You need ladies to see to you—your hair, nails, jewels. We need to fix your sword. For the coronation, you'll need a crown. One that you'll actually wear. And after," I took a steadying breath, keeping firm, as compassion wasn't what she needed from me right then, "you'll have to sit on the High Throne."

So much there that she hated. Better to lay out all the pain at once. At least I'd accurately predicted what would disturb her most in that list, making up for my miss on the coronation gown. Her hand had fallen to her sword hilt, where the missing jewel had been. That hurt the worst.

"We could find another topaz," I told her quietly. "Something that might look the same."

Her expression shuttered. "No need. I have it. That's enough."

"One of the rubies then. We could prize them from the crown jewels."

Ami and Andi followed the exchange with great interest. Had they known that Ursula had stashed away Salena's rubies in her wardrobe all those years? Ursula wondered, too, her gaze going to them, each in turn, measuring. "Yes," she decided. "Prize the jewels from their settings. One for my sword, the others equally divided between Ami and Andi. If that's allowable within your rules, librarian."

Not my rules, those of the law, as the queen's jewels technically belonged to the station, not a person, but I let it go. "The crown?" I prodded.

"I won't wear his." She glared at me in defiance, reminding me of the adolescent girl she'd been in those first years after Salena died, full of anger and anguish.

"Fine. You should have your own. Whatever seems right to you. The same with the throne."

"Truly?" She mulled that over, seeming, for the first time since I'd arrived, hopeful.

"I'd recommend it, in fact. It's past time to do away with the empty thrones. There should be just one. As rulers of their own kingdoms, Queen Andromeda, King Rayfe, and Queen Amelia hold equal rank to any of the kings and queens of the kingdoms under your rule—they have their own realms, their own concerns—they should not be sitting next to the High Throne unless you plan to give all the kingdoms a chair beside you." Once Salena died, Uorsin had kept hers ostentatiously present and empty. As they departed, Andi and Ami had left theirs similarly abandoned. A sight that reminded all who viewed them of attrition and loss. Not what we wanted at all.

"I dreamed…" Ursula sounded uncharacteristically uncertain.

"What?" Everyone else stayed quiet, listening.

She shook herself. Looking around at the people gathered. The ones she loved and trusted the most.

"It's not just about you," Andi said, in a gentle tone. "The visions our mother gave you, she gave to all of us."

"You think so?" Ursula sounded more like herself, the pragmatic skeptic.

"Yes," Ami chimed in, emphatic. "Did you dream of a

throne? Tell us about it."

"When she told me what to do, how to end it all, yes, Salena sat on a throne." Ursula didn't much like talking about things not grounded in the real world of flesh and blood, but her voice gained strength as we listened. "It was carved of wood, with intricate vines and flowers. It stood alone." She cast a glance over her shoulder at Harlan, who simply smiled.

"You know I prefer to stand rather than sit," was all he said.

"I have some artisans who could carve such a thing in short time," Rayfe offered. Everyone turned to him in surprise and he affected shock. "What? I support my heart-sister." His grin turned wolfish. "In exchange for heavy concessions for Annfwn."

"I've found precedent for that," I offered, less certain here. "We can sit down with the various original treaties among the Twelve—they varied depending on the process of'—I had to clear my throat of old grief and tension—"ah, acquisition."

"Annfwn will not be acquired." Rayfe had gone deadly serious, with a lethal edge. Though he remained in human form, the predator looked out of his eyes, making my coward's heart skip a beat.

~ 8 ~

"IT'S NOT A question," Ursula answered with her own edge, taking over for my blunder and doing what she did best. "Your borders are open and we are all bedfellows whether you like it or not. All that remains is to sort out the legal details."

Rayfe hadn't moved, but he seemed to shimmer, the way Tala did moments before they shifted. Though she sat with her back to him, Andi must have sensed it because she narrowed her eyes at Ursula. "Stop baiting him." She said it mildly, but the words carried her own brand of threat.

Ursula held up her hands, a peacemaking gesture, but the frustrated furrows on her brow belied it. "Apologies, King Rayfe." She seemed about to say something more, but sighed out a sharp breath instead and turned to me. "We'll table this debate until the librarian has finished. What else?"

It hit me, the question, the implicit trust in it. The future High Queen of the Thirteen Kingdoms not only listened to my advice but would follow it. Exhilarating, yes. Also daunting for a small cat, in a room with six wolves, all focused on me. Even Ami, with her lush beauty, possessed a ferocious heart. Enviable, their strength and courage. I took a deep breath. *Focus on the immediate.* I, at least, had knowledge, and it had always served me well.

"Two more things." I hated to throw more discord into the already tense conversation, but they had to think about these things now. "Because you can only declare one heir, you need to pick which twin it will be. And you need to decide who will perform the coronation."

All looked to Ami at that. She took the easier question first. "Who crowned Uorsin? I don't think I ever knew."

"High Priest Kir." I let that sit a moment with them, not at all surprised by their varying expressions of dismay and Ami's outright groan.

"Why is that a problem?" Harlan inquired. "Will he not agree?"

"He might have," Ami replied with a rueful smile, "if we could find him and if I hadn't deposed him as the head of Glorianna's church after sending him on that quest to nowhere. What's most odd is that he's never returned. Do you suppose a monster ate him?"

Though Ursula didn't exactly crack a smile at that, her eyes lit with a hint of amused satisfaction. "I warned you that your actions would have long-ranging consequences."

"You didn't stop me," Ami retorted. "I thought maybe you weren't even paying attention."

"I always pay attention. I held no great love for Kir and, as you know, I look to Danu, not Glorianna. It seemed meet to leave that to you. However"—she clicked her tongue, thinking—"it certainly drops a problem in our laps now."

"Who *is* head of Glorianna's church?" Andi asked.

"Me." Ami smiled apologetically through her chagrin. "Ursula's right. I guess I didn't think through the ramifications." She cast a glance over her shoulder at Ash. His scarred face remained somber, making the look in his uncanny green eyes all that much more radiant in contrast, as if he gazed at the sun. "Though it was worth it and I'd do it again. It made it easier to effect important changes."

"It didn't occur to me, either, at the time," I told her, by way of support and apology. Instead I'd assisted her with enthusiasm, in full agreement with resolving the corruption in the church that had wounded so many like Ash. "But you can't crown your own sister High Queen."

"Uorsin declared Glorianna's church as the official one of the Twelve, for reasons I can only guess at," Ursula mused. "If we agree with Ami's suggestion that we officially return all three goddesses to equal footing, could we have a ceremony with a priest or priestess each of Glorianna, Danu, and Moranu?"

"That's how we were married," Andi glanced over her shoulder at Rayfe, who gazed back at her with some deep emotion. Wed on yet another battlefield soaked in blood. I'd liked him for her then, with his wild blue eyes and carefully controlled sense of danger. Not unlike Andi herself.

"Truly?" Ursula shook her head. "I don't think I knew that." Because she hadn't been there, it went without saying, as she'd been leading Uorsin's armies to stop the wedding. "Would that work, Dafne? And would I have to declare Glorianna's worship no longer the official one and elevate the others?"

I opened my mouth, but Ami beat me to it. "No, don't do that. Being crowned by representatives of all three will say the same thing, without sending all the priests of Glorianna into fits."

"Moranu and Danu don't have the same internal hierarchies in their temples," I pointed out. "You could ask for someone special from each, the oldest within traveling distance or some such. That lets you out of having the head of Glorianna's church involved."

"Does this make you High Priestess?" Andi demanded of Ami, who flushed.

"I'll take care of it," she muttered.

"Probably wise," Ursula agreed. "And Astar and Stella?"

Ami stared back evenly. "You tell me. But I should point out that I owe Avonlidgh an heir, also. I won't break that promise to Hugh."

"Uorsin wanted Astar for his heir."

"And Andromeda would claim Stella for hers," Rayfe inserted meaningfully.

"You know, you both might have babies of your own," Ami pointed out with a certain malicious delight, casting a significant glance at Ursula's lean waist and fluttering her lashes. "I know it's not for lack of creating the opportunity."

To my surprise, Ursula did not tease back, but tensed, going brittle. With a long look at her, Harlan spoke up. "We've agreed that any children we might have together will not inherit the High Throne."

Silence, prickly and chill, fell over the room. Andi studied them both, her eyes going to fog as they did when she glimpsed visions of another place and time.

"Because you're not married?" Ami asked. "Simple—marry the man already. Make an honest mercenary of him."

"I cannot marry a prince of Dasnaria," Ursula said, slowly spacing out the words, as if speaking to an idiot. "No more than *you*, as the Queen of Avonlidgh, can marry an ex-convict. No disrespect, Ash."

He shrugged, pitted face difficult to read. "I *am* an ex-convict. Though it would be most welcome if you would get yourself crowned and correct some of the laws that would have me sent back to prison, should anyone else discover the fact."

"I haven't forgotten what I promised," Ursula returned in her deliberately mild tone that meant she was more on edge than ever.

"All we need to decide at this moment," I inserted into the rising tension, "is an interim heir. Should more babies … develop, we can revisit the debate."

Ursula flicked a glance at me, raising her brows at my attempt to avoid the thorny issue. I sighed and dipped my chin in acknowledgment of her silent point, much as I hated it.

"Her Highness is likely correct. With Dasnaria neither an ally nor an enemy, we cannot afford to create such an alliance, especially so early in Ursula's reign. At least formally." I gave Harlan an apologetic half smile, but his implacable expression did not alter.

"It is of no concern to me." He spoke to Ursula, though she didn't look at him, with the air of a man who's repeated the same thing numerous times. Likely he had. "Likewise, I highly doubt Dasnaria will concern herself with us. My brothers wrote me off as not useless years ago. I'm sure they give no more thought to me than I do to them."

Andi startled, her eyes flying wide. She covered it quickly, but not before Ursula saw it, too. "What do you see?" she asked softly, nearly hesitant.

Andi shook her head. "Nothing clear."

"Something."

"Just… I think Dafne is right. We need to put things in order quickly." She firmed her mouth over saying more. A bad sign. Perhaps I could get her to talk privately.

I cleared my throat, preparing to herd my roomful of restless predators back to the decision at hand, but Ursula beat me to it.

"All right then. Astar cannot be heir to both Avonlidgh and the High Throne," she said. "By the same token, Stella cannot be heir to both Avonlidgh and Annfwn."

"I should have had triplets," Ami grumbled, then shot Ash a saucy grin. "Want to try for more?"

"They wouldn't be legitimate heirs," Ursula reminded her. "You'd have to marry to produce legal heirs."

"I know that, but I'm not marrying anyone but Ash," Ami fired back.

"Then, like me, you won't marry."

"Besides," Ash remarked, a whisper of a laugh under the gravel in his voice, "I haven't offered."

"Oh hush." Ami scowled at his amusement. "I'd command you to do it. What's the point of being queen if I can't do whatever I want?"

"Ursula is free to marry another," Harlan put in, perfectly neutral.

Ursula turned in her chair to give him an incredulous look. "No."

"You owe me no vow such as I made to you. Your priority has to be the best choice for those under your rule. If an alliance becomes important, you should be free to make it."

"And you'd just stand by?"

He simply touched the backs of his fingers to his forehead, in the intimate salute he gave only to Ursula. "The *Elskastholrr* binds me to you, not the other way around."

"I said it back to you," she replied and his stern expression melted with emotion almost embarrassing to witness.

"I know. Which I treasure, but without the *Skablykrr*, it lacks the same weight. You are, and will remain, free of obligation to me." He cast me a somber look. "Lady Mailloux should be aware of this truth, to advise you accordingly."

"Should I also know what it means?" I asked, somewhat faintly as I tried to assimilate this information.

"It's not a secret," Harlan replied, gaze falling to Ursula as she turned her back to him and scowled at the table, "though—for the very reason I brought it up—it might be best if the information not go beyond the people in this room. "The *Elskastholrr* is a tradition that goes back many centuries, in the school of *Skablykrr*, which teaches a philosophical and martial system. It's a pledge that a man gives a woman, to devote himself to her and only to her, for the rest of his life."

~ 9 ~

A SH WHISTLED LOW and long. Only Andi seemed unsurprised. Quite possibly such a vow contained a magical component that she could sense.

"Only men to women?" Ami asked. "Not the other way around?" Ash made a disparaging sound and she flicked her fingertips at him.

Harlan shook his head slowly. "Dasnarian women are different. They do not train to fight or take this schooling such as the men do. I've come to see this as Dasnaria's loss, in truth."

"I've never read about the *Elskastholrr*," I ventured. And I'd been reading quite a bit about Dasnaria since the arrival of Harlan and his Vervaldr, not to mention Illyria.

"You wouldn't have, not directly, as it's not to be recorded in any permanent form. However, you'll find references if you research Dasnarian love ballads and tales."

"Particularly the tragic ones," Ursula snapped, clearly seething over the situation.

Harlan only smiled easily at the back of her head. "All in the eye of the beholder, Your Highness." The way he spoke her title sounded like a profound expression of love.

One I had to look away from, as I felt like an intruder on something too intimate for witnesses. "I will look into that.

Thank you for telling me. We will have to address the subject of marriage eventually." I met Ursula's glare, holding my ground. "There will be offers. You know that."

"Then know this." She relaxed, losing her anger in the certainty of the decision she'd come to. Standing, she turned to face Harlan, a slim blade of a woman before his bulk. "I might not have the training or authority to make the vow that you have, but I can make my own pledges, based on my own beliefs. There will never be another for me. No matter what."

"You don't have to prove anything to me, my hawk."

"Maybe I have something to prove to myself then. I'll abdicate the crown before I marry another."

Though they didn't touch, only held each other's gazes, the moment stretched out, humming with intimate power.

Andi shook back her hair, coughing lightly to break the moment. "Probably something else that shouldn't leave this room."

Ursula seated herself again, a hint of self-conscious color on her cheeks at having exposed herself, but she held firm. "It's good that you all know where I stand on this."

"It figures," Ami remarked in a dry voice, "that the woman who refrained from all courtship would fall so hard and deep."

"Of course, Essla never did do anything by halves," Andi answered her.

"I'm sitting right here," Ursula reminded them, but a slight smile curved her lips.

I cleared my throat, yet again, and tapped the scroll before me, where I had carefully *not* noted anything about the promises between our future High Queen and her unofficial consort. Though I might write it down privately for myself later. I intended to keep a journal of these days and perhaps later write a history. My own contribution to archiving this era in the Twelve

Kingdoms. Such important information should not be completely lost. I had made no vows as Harlan had, to keep the *Elskastholrr* unwritten. Nor would I promise to keep it secret— my allegiance to recording and preserving information took precedence.

"Designating who would be in line to take the High Throne remains on the table." I brought them back to the matter at hand.

"Andi and Rayfe will name Stella their heir for the time being and Astar will remain Avonlidgh's," Ursula said, swiftly enough to make me realize she'd long since decided on that course and had let the conversation spin out for her own reasons. Perhaps she'd planned all along to make the declaration of her intentions toward Harlan clear to at least the people in that room.

Andi looked to Rayfe, who inclined his head, deferring to her. She then exchanged glances with Ami, who nodded.

"I thank you, and the Tala thank you," Andi told her, "for the gift of your daughter."

"Don't think I'll let you forget it," Ami replied with some of her usual sass, but her eyes glistened with emotion.

I noted down the decision, a bit surprised to find myself similarly moved. History in the making. "And the High Throne?"

Ursula's narrow mouth quirked in malicious amusement. "Guess what, Queen Andromeda?"

Andi's face went blank with shock. "Moranu take you, no!"

"And here I thought you saw the future so clearly," Ursula commented in a bland tone that nevertheless needled her sister over whatever it was that she'd seen at the mention of Dasnaria and refused to describe. "You have ever been second in line for the High Throne after me. It takes no magic to predict that.”

The argument continued for a while after that, but Ursula's logic was sound and Andi couldn't wriggle out of it. Particularly when Ursula pointed out that having Andi and Stella in line for the High Throne would follow the path Salena had set. Andi finally conceded after taking time to "meditate on the matter," which meant she'd looked as far as she could into the future and saw no likelihood that she'd ever be forced to take the High Throne.

After hours more of discussion, which had everyone sitting at the table by the end, the detritus of food and drink around us, Ursula and Rayfe had hammered out a treaty. Andi stayed out of that discussion for the most part, occasionally flicking me an amused glance as we watched the pair of them fence over details, a competition they both relished.

Ash took a surprisingly active role in the finer points of citizenship. He had ideas—good ones—for repatriating the Tala prisoners and other exiles scattered throughout the Twelve, and he began documenting them for me in surprisingly well-educated script. Wherever he'd been before his incarceration, he'd had a better upbringing than many of the Tala part-blood brethren he fought to aid. Or perhaps after prison. Something that sparked an idea in me.

In the end, they agreed to Annfwn becoming an independent ally, by way of Rayfe's marriage to a Princess of the Realm. Truly ironic, that the clash that had set so many of our troubles in motion now provided a convenient structure for creating peace in that direction.

"It sets precedent," I commented as I finished noting the points to have the agreement formally drafted.

"We're not going through that again," Ursula carefully didn't look at Harlan. We all knew we'd have trouble ahead, with the various rulers of the now-Thirteen Kingdoms looking to gain the more enviable independent ally status by wedding Ursula or Ami.

"I won't apologize." Rayfe had tied his hair back with a leather thong. "The welfare of Annfwn has to come first for me, and that means having independent control of our resources."

"We've agreed, haven't we? It's signed and done. We'll deal with the ramifications as they arise." Ursula had her eyes on Andi, who looked tired. "Speaking of resources—how much is the change in the barrier draining you? It's still there, isn't it? Speak honestly, as we've aired so many other secrets in this room."

Andi cast an assessing glance at Rayfe, who lolled back in his chair, returning her gaze with a wealth of meaning behind it.

Andi smiled wryly and nodded. "It's there, but much farther away."

"How far?" Ursula wanted to know.

"It's not as if I can draw it on a map," Andi retorted. "It would be like trying to explain to you how far my toes are from my ears. It's a feeling."

Ursula waited without comment and Andi sighed. "Fine, yes. It's much more draining this way. Perhaps once I get back to…" She flicked a glance around the table, editing out mention of the Heart, no doubt. "The center of Annfwn, it will be better."

"Then you should go home," Ursula told her, face hardening when Andi opened her mouth to protest. "You're no good to me half dead."

Andi fired. "I will see you crowned. I'm not abandoning you."

"Nor am I." Ami jumped in. "There's been enough of you

facing things alone."

Ursula looked between them, a rare soft emotion relaxing her shoulders. "I'm not facing anything alone. I know that now. I have Harlan and Dafne—formidable defenders for different enemies—and the librarian has it correct. You must take up your roles in your own kingdoms. I know where to find you. More, I know you'll come the moment I call, as I would for you."

A circle of connection hummed between the three sisters, old as birth. I almost expected Salena to walk into the room, smiling at her daughters, proud of what they'd constructed from the puzzle pieces she'd left behind. At least she'd given me a small part to play, too, and I would see it through. Their sisterhood would never include me. Fate had made me an orphan and that wouldn't change. But I could be close to what made them extraordinary, help them along in what ways I could.

And write the histories after.

"Besides," I inserted into the speaking silence, "we won't have the coronation for at least a month. There's too much to do. You can plan to return."

Ursula gave me a look of horror. "A month—to plan a party?"

"An occasion of state that will launch your reign." I held firm. "We're doing this right. I'll detail a timeline and then we can announce the date."

Andi threw up her hands, as if warding off the prospect. "I'm convinced. You don't need any other help."

"Coward," Ursula muttered, while Ami only grinned.

"I'll work with the barrier and we'll come back for the coronation. I'll also look into making it rain in Aerron," Andi soothed her, then rolled her eyes the moment Ursula looked away.

Ursula caught it anyway and pointed a finger at her. "Soft, soaking rains. Too much at once with the ground so hard and we'll have flooding."

"I know, I know." Andi rolled her eyes again. "That's why I want to approach the problem slowly and delicately, where I have the best connection and control." She looked to Rayfe. "We'll depart in the morning?"

He nodded, a look of relief crossing his face, and took her hand.

"We'll go tomorrow, too, since things are handled here," Ami said, throwing me a nod of appreciation. "I'll go first to Castle Avonlidgh to set things to rights in the kingdom from there. Do a formal naming of Stella, then tour around a bit and let the people see Astar and Stella. That will keep us closer to Ordnung to return in a month's time for the coronation."

"But not to Windroven," Ursula inserted smoothly.

"Of course to Windroven," Ami replied, setting her chin. "Castle Avonlidgh may be the capital, but Windroven is the ancestral seat of Hugh's family. The people there deserve to see their heir. And it's my home."

"Reports indicate the volcano at Windroven is becoming active. You're not going there."

"Is that an order?" Ami demanded.

Ursula simply gazed back. "A favor. To ease my mind. Until we know more. Please."

"You're easier to refuse when you're dictatorial," Ami grumped. "Fine, but I want any information your scouts bring back and I'm sending some of my own to find out more. If the volcano is dangerous, everyone should evacuate."

It made me sad to think of it, the arcanely beautiful castle built into the ancient volcano on the cliffs overlooking the sea, the rich farmland—all in danger of obliteration.

"Agreed," Ursula told her gravely, speaking High Queen to Queen. "You and your people will have whatever support you need from Ordnung."

"And from Annfwn." Andi side-eyed Rayfe, who only narrowed his eyes at her. "I'm sure Rayfe has as many fond memories of Windroven as I do," she added mischievously.

He laughed then, and picked up her hand to kiss her palm. "Well-played, my queen. Yes," he said to Ami, and nodded also to Ash, "send to us for whatever you need. The Tala owe the people of Avonlidgh a debt, for both the losses we caused—and the treasure we gained."

Andi flushed, giving him a speaking look. I suspected Rayfe had won that round after all.

~ 10 ~

"**A**SH—COULD I HAVE a moment of your time?" I nodded to Ami, who raised her brows at me. The other four had already left, discussing something about the journey to Annfwn. "With Your Highness's permission, naturally."

"Dafne," she chided. "You know full well I can't make this obstinate ox of a man do anything one way or another." She gave him a saucy wink. "But don't stay away too long or I might be asleep."

A slight smile twisted the scar that bisected Ash's lip. "Knowing how long it takes you to brush your hair the requisite number of strokes, I'm sure I have plenty of time."

"Cheeky." She stood on tiptoes to give him a lingering kiss, one that made his eyes burn as he gazed in her direction long after her trim form disappeared out the door.

With an apparent effort of will, he dragged his attention back to me, smile going rueful that he'd forgotten I waited. "Apologies, librarian. One day perhaps she won't sear my thoughts into little pieces with one kiss."

"I hope that day never comes," I said, in all sincerity. "What you two have is precious—and enviable."

"I suppose that's true. Certainly not something I ever imagined I could have." He looked thoughtful, then shook it off.

"How may I be of service to you, librarian?"

I hesitated. Ash wasn't as obviously a warrior to avoid tangling with, like Rayfe or Harlan—and I put little store by his criminal conviction, as I knew having Tala blood would have been enough to put him in prison—but he had his own edge of danger. That of a very private man, the lone predator who avoided confrontation but decisively ended any he was forced into.

"I don't wish to trespass on private matters, which is why I wanted to pose my questions to you alone. However, I fear that even asking may be… inappropriate."

His corrugated face tended to be forbidding and now it settled into stark lines. "Ask. If I don't wish to answer, I won't."

Afraid I'd already offended him, I took a deep breath. I had a job to do. "All right then. Were you ever truly one of the White Monks and, if so, can you tell me how to contact them?"

I'd surprised him, the bright green of his eyes flashing briefly before he turned his face away to look out the window. When he'd first come to Windroven in the company of High Priest Kir, Ash had worn the robes of one of the near mythical White Monks. The few whispers and tales of them indicated they were almost cultlike in their dedication to the worship of Glorianna— and totally separate from the official Church. What I'd been able to uncover about them indicated that the monks spent the first three years of service under a strict vow of silence. The name of the order reflected the stillness and purity they believed silencing the voice and mind brought, the color of their robes deriving from that concept, rather than the reverse. Many of the White Monks apparently never spoke again.

Obviously, Ash did. But then, he'd also used the position to gain admittance to Ami's entourage, in the hopes she'd take him into Annfwn with her. I'd never known how much of his role had been subterfuge and Ami had never said. It was between them and I wouldn't have asked, without the current need.

"Why do you wonder?" He finally asked, raspy voice fogged with some dark emotion.

"I'm sorry. I truly did not mean to distress you."

He met my eyes again, rueful humor in them. "Am I distressed? No. Simply…perhaps swamped with old memories. This is not something I discuss easily or often."

"I'm sorry," I said again. "Never mind. I'll find another way to contact them."

"Don't be ridiculous." He shook off whatever had enshrouded him. "You're thinking for the coronation."

"Yes."

"Why the White Monks?"

"I'm not certain it's the correct choice—that's part of why I'm asking you. From what I understand, the order is very old, predating most of the worship we associate with Glorianna today. I can't think of any other part of the Church that will not bear something of Uorsin's taint. While I was in Annfwn I found an old tale about Talifa, the first Queen of the Tala, from whom the Tala draw their name, according to the legend. And who founded a scholarly society to study Moranu's sister, Glorianna."

He stared at me, arrested. "I didn't know that story had made it out of the order."

"Then you were one of them."

"I was." His eyes darkened in reflection. "They took me in, hid me. Taught me. Three years of silence meant I never had to speak of where—or who—I'd been. That kind of quiet… well, it allowed me to leave behind the beast prison had made me into. They allowed me to be as much of a man as I'll ever be."

"A far better man than most."

He laughed his soundless rasp. "Better than I once was, which is a beginning. I think you are wise in this. The order is… much closer to the old magic of the numinous than I've seen in any other part of Glorianna's Church. I will write a letter of introduction to my old mentor and give you the direction. The rest will be up to you, to do the convincing."

A difficult task, to be sure.

After I left Ash, I found Andi lingering over wine with Ursula, while a minstrel played. In the flickering shadows of the firelight, they more resembled each other than not. Especially in the curve of the smiles they welcomed me with. Both of them relaxed and sleepy now. Ursula, however, read in one glance that I arrived with a purpose.

"Dare I hope you want something from my sister and not me?" She asked, sounding convinced otherwise.

"Actually yes, Your Highness. I'm hoping for a moment of Queen Andromeda's time."

Ursula uncoiled to her feet with smooth alacrity. "She's back to using titles, which means I'm seizing this reprieve."

"Now who's the coward?" Andi scowled at her.

"The better part of valor," Ursula cheerfully agreed. "I'll see you off in the morning. Have my chair, librarian."

I took it, because it was the only seat close enough to keep my conversation with Andi private, though the symbolism made me uneasy. I might be moving in rarified circles, consorting with queens and kings, but it would be a fatal error to imagine myself equal to any of them, or able to take their places in any way.

Andi regarded me warily, which helped ease my apprehension, that a sorceress as powerful as she would treat me as a threat. Humorous, indeed.

"My first request is a simple one," I said, taking the easy path. "Remember the Tala man, the shaman who married you and Rayfe in Moranu's name?"

"It's a moment that sticks in my memory, yes," she replied drily.

"Could he or his… group be contacted to perform Moranu's third of the coronation?"

Andi looked interested. "And thereby demonstrate Tala support for the new High Queen, with Moranu's blessing? Clever of you, librarian. Draft your missive, send your messenger to me in Annfwn, and I'll make the contact."

"Thank you."

The silence stretched out. She'd learned a great deal as Queen of the Tala. Once she would have prodded me. Now she simply waited, her stormy eyes shadowed, making me speak first.

"What did you see about Dasnaria?" I asked it baldly, though in a quiet tone that wouldn't carry over the music. Andi began to shake her head and I gave her my sternest look. "Don't tell me it was nothing of import. You said we need to put things in order, so I'm doing that. Before *what* happens?"

Her eyes glinted with an edge of silver. "Why would I tell you and not my elder sister, who is, by the way, far more intimidating, so don't try that with me."

"Because Her Highness and I are not the same person. She has enough to think about without planning future battles she can't yet act on, particularly one as fraught as something tied up with Harlan. It's my job to anticipate the trials to come and do what I can to prepare so that when the time comes, she has what she needs to act. What did you see?"

She huffed out a sigh, reached for a clean goblet and poured for us both. "It's not that simple. It's not like reading a book, with the history nicely linear and laid out in detail."

"What is it like?" I hadn't meant to ask, but curiosity overtook me.

"It's… more like dream images. Do you ever get recurring dreams—yes? It's like those, the way the details might change but the core images remain the same. And I'm awake." She grimaced.

"These 'core' images—they're the events most likely to occur."

"Usually. Though key elements can change. For example, I saw the moment Ursula killed Hugh, for months before it happened. Everything the same each time—the snow, the crimson blood staining the white—but until that exact second, it was always Rayfe who died, not Hugh."

Shadows haunted her face, much as I imagined the guilt did.

"You didn't plan it. You couldn't have. It happened so fast—you couldn't have consciously chosen for Ami's husband to die instead of yours."

"Maybe yes, maybe no?" She tapped a finger on her goblet. "I made sure Rayfe didn't die, which means I altered the course of events because of what I'd seen. Another good man died as a direct result, no matter whose fault." Her stormy gaze met mine. "I'm very careful with what I do about what I see."

"This is your gift—your mother's gift. It's yours to use as she used it."

She huffed a humorless laugh. "I am not Salena. I can't follow the complex interweaving of possible events the way she must have. I seem to see days, maybe months. At most a year. She looked decades into the future, possibly farther."

"She trained in it all her life. You've barely come into your own. Every time I see you, I can feel the magic is stronger."

"You think so?" She eyed me, a hint showing of the skittish girl she'd been, slipping through the halls, keeping to herself. "You once compared that feeling to an insect crawling on you."

"A beautiful and exotic one," I corrected her, with amused chagrin at my audacity in having told her that, in my struggle to give her the best analogy. "Salena was the same way. Tell me this: is a month enough time to be ready?"

She looked through me, at something only she could see, then nodded judiciously. "It should be. Events are already in motion. Have been since Uorsin fell and the barrier moved. It's all tied together. But the core image always includes Ursula wearing a crown. If that changes, I'll send a message."

I ground my teeth against the frustration. "Can you tell me anything more about this image? I already know it has to do with what Harlan said, about Dasnaria not concerning herself with us. I won't speak of it—just so I can know and do the research."

Andi considered me, then leaned close, dark hair spilling over her shoulders. "Secrecy then. Salena trusted you, so will I. There are four men, exotically armored. Tall, broad, and fair-haired. Ursula crowned, on her throne."

I caught my breath and she nodded.

"I don't know them, but they are Dasnarians, not Vervaldr. In the great hall at Ordnung."

THEY LEFT IN the morning, going in opposite directions with their vastly different entourages.

Andi refused to say more than she had and no one could move her once she dug in her heels. Something all three sisters shared and I'd long since learned not to fight their stubbornness head on. At least I knew to pursue my studies of Dasnaria, in what little spare time fell to me.

I had a month to make sure Ursula had secured the throne before this challenge arrived.

After that, we might be looking to her to save us from it.

~ 11 ~

"**I** OBJECT TO this coronation."

Prince Stefan, of course, petitioned to speak the moment the date for the coronation was announced in informal court. As his words echoed through the great hall, I bitterly regretted having stayed awake all night, as the debate promised to be both difficult and endless.

However, we'd decided the missives had to be sent for priests or priestesses to perform the coronation as a top priority, given how much time it might take for the messages to reach my far-flung choices and for them to then travel to Ordnung.

Or for alternates to be selected, if my plan did not work.

In my hopes of recruiting acolytes from the old orders, ones that resonated with the magic that formed our new reality, I'd made my task exponentially more difficult. Particularly to put in writing. Not an easy question to get at, when for so many years all had scrupulously followed Uorsin's decree that magic was a myth. I couldn't exactly write out, "now that Her Highness Ursula has performed a blood sacrifice, creating a new contract with the land via magical resonance that we don't fully understand but need confirmed in similar style with an official coronation, would you send one of your oldest, most venerated practitioners on a long, possibly dangerous journey to perform a rite we haven't decided on yet?"

Ursula, with a certain carefree relish, had told me to do as I saw fit, since it was all my plan anyway. So I'd composed, rewritten, and revised the wording all night. I hadn't paid attention to the time, partly out of habit. I'd long had the freedom and inclination to pursue projects into the wee hours, satisfying my own compulsion to see them through. Nights were quiet and let me concentrate without interruption.

I was also feeling the pressure to get this coronation right. What did I know of magic and recruiting the good will of goddesses—or of monkish hermits and wild-haired shamans? And yet there I was, working the alchemy of words to make it happen.

And thus I had not fully considered the implications of my new position, which meant that there would be no slipping away from court, informal or not, for a much-needed nap. My messengers had departed—Zynda herself carrying the one to Annfwn—but I'd failed to consider that with those missives stating the planned date, we'd have to also publicly announce the timing of the coronation, and that would be like throwing bloody meat into the kennel of starving hounds that was the restless court of Ordnung.

I mentally sighed at Stefan's immediate resistance, but better to begin the fight now, in order to end it in time. Just as well to get Duranor handled first, as Stefan's obstinacy and considerable armies—which remained encamped outside Ordnung's walls, not incidentally—posed the biggest threats.

Ursula, looking regal indeed in her new court gear, sitting on the throne she'd always used as heir, regarded him with cool disdain. I might know of her private doubts, but she showed none of them to the world. Admirable control. If nothing else, having a father like Uorsin had taught her that.

"You have no grounds—or power—to object. My ascension to the High Throne is not a subject for debate. Unless Duranor wishes to take up arms against the combined might of her sister kingdoms, including the Tala of Annfwn, once our vicious enemy, now our ally?"

He wanted to, that much showed clear in the tense rebellion of his stance, the angry clench of his jaw. We also all knew his forces, while they could cause us serious hurt, would be unlikely to prevail in anything but a victory that would only decimate our fragile recovery even further. And no one wanted to meet the Tala in battle. The war to prevent Andi and Rayfe's wedding loomed large in our memories still, refreshed by the horrors people had seen during the liberation of Ordnung. The demons, wizards, and shapeshifters might be our new allies, but it would take many years for the average citizen to feel comfortable with that.

They did trust their future High Queen, though. If nothing else, by freeing everyone in Ordnung from the grim fate they'd seen so many suffer, Ursula had gained heroic status and won deeply felt loyalty. Uorsin had berated and abandoned them. Ursula had saved them. People finally felt hope for the future. No one wanted more conflict.

The good will wouldn't last forever—people have short memories and never read the history books as they should—but it certainly helped at the moment.

"Duranor has no need to take up arms." Stefan pretended to cool logic, though he couldn't quite match Ursula's ice. They were of an age, but she'd endured far hotter fires than he. "I question your right to rule on legal grounds. Or do you plan to follow in your father's footsteps and simply impose another version of his tyranny upon us?"

"I impose nothing. You—or rather your king, *Prince* Stefan—signed treaties agreeing to be subject to the laws of the Twelve Kingdoms. Laws that support my coronation as High Queen."

"Duranor signed under duress," he ground out through clenched jaws.

"Regardless of the past—something neither of us can alter—it is a bond that *you* cannot dissolve legally."

"I put that back in your lap, Your Highness. Legality is exactly what I speak to." He was working his way around to springing whatever trap he had planned. I pretended to be involved with the scroll before me, while surreptitiously keeping an eye on both him and the assembly. Much depended on who sided with him. Ambassador Laurenne of Aerron carried great sway in the court. While she had a fondness for Ursula, she'd also been colluding with Stefan. Not out of love for Duranor, but for the promise of water in the form of an aqueduct between their lands. Andi couldn't bring rain soon enough. It would be difficult to blame Laurenne for choosing a known probability over a vague, magical possibility.

Stefan posed, letting the murmurs of background conversation settle into silence, waiting for the attention of all before he dropped his axe blade of doubt. "Uorsin passed to Glorianna's arms without naming an heir." He piously drew the Circle of Glorianna in the air, his face wearing a sorrowful mask I knew to be insincere. No one mourned Uorsin, and Duranor least of all. "Therefore Duranor's treaty, all of our treaties, which were with the High King and his nonexistent heir, died with him."

Goddesses take him. What could he know to make such a claim?

Ambassador Laurenne stood, her ancient face serene. I held my breath, praying to all three goddesses for her to be on our side. If possible, the assembly stilled even more. If she had been respected before, for her dedicated and single-minded fight to save her realm, the fact that she'd managed to survive Illyria's rampages made her a hero in her own right.

"You're laboring under a misapprehension, Prince Stefan," she said, and I let the breath out carefully, wary of hoping too soon. "I myself witnessed the ceremony during which High King Uorsin named his eldest daughter Ursula as his heir when she was but twelve years of age. I'm sure it was duly recorded." She glanced to me at my table, so I held up the scroll I'd kept close to hand. At least I'd planned ahead that much.

"Indeed, Ambassador. I have it here, if any care to examine it. There are also copies in the libraries of the seats of all the Twelve." Or should be. I made a note to send a copy to Annfwn, too, wishing I'd thought of it soon enough to send with Zynda. Not that anyone there would ever look at it. Still.

"Oh yes, Your Highness, we've seen *that*." Stefan dismissed the scroll, looking far too pleased, the way he spoke Ursula's title making even that sound dubious. "I'm talking about how High King Uorsin *dis*inherited you. The day you returned without Prince Astar, the babe he had declared right here in open court would be his new heir, should the babe be a boy. A declaration we *all* witnessed." He bowed in Laurenne's direction with a mocking smile, then aimed it at Harlan. "Even your current paramour would have to admit to that; as he stood at the High King's elbow."

Ursula didn't show any more emotion than she had thus far, but I knew her well enough to see his words had affected her. Worse, Harlan's usual neutral mask cracked slightly. He always stood where he could keep one eye on her and one on anyone who might approach, but his focus had gone entirely to Ursula. Not because of the implied insult, I thought. He knew something that I didn't.

"My father discussed naming Prince Astar as his heir, yes." Ursula sounded coolly disinterested, parrying the attack without apparent effort. "We all heard him say so numerous times, beginning when Lady Zevondeth first predicted that the child Queen Amelia would bear would be a boy."

Stefan drew himself up to speak, but she held up a hand to stop him.

"As correct as Lady Zevondeth's prophecy turned out to be, so too was Queen Andromeda's: that a girl would be born."

"I never heard any such prediction that—"

"No, because you have never been privy to the discussions of the royal family." That stung him and I had to suppress a smile. "The Three blessed my sister with both a son and a daughter. Once the twins have been presented to the people of Avonlidgh, as is the proper order of things"—she inclined her head toward the Avonlidgh ambassador, newly arrived at court following the failure of his former king's rebellion, who bowed graciously in return—"they will return to Ordnung to be formally acknowledged as my niece and nephew. His Majesty, the late High King Uorsin, however, passed into Glorianna's arms"—here she truly impressed me by mimicking the sentiment without a flicker of sarcasm—"without formally declaring either babe as his heir, nor did he disinherit me. I remain Uorsin's heir."

"Because you murdered him!" An anonymous voice shouted from the back.

"Shut up," another hissed, far too loudly, "or she'll do for you, too!"

Stefan let the paranoid murmurs roll around, smiling point-edly at Ursula, until they subsided into quiet attention again. I braced for his next salvo.

"You claim the High King did not disinherit you, Your Highness." Stefan spread his hands in apparent bewilderment. "So how did it happen that the Heir's Circlet returned to his possession and from his, into Illyria's?"

I fervently wished I possessed Ursula's knack for showing no reaction.

Uorsin *had* taken it from her, I realized with shock as force-ful as a hard fall. It had been that same day we'd returned, when she'd met with him privately after the feast. She'd suffered a blow to her cheek, with a bruised and bleeding cut on her temple where her circlet usually sat. It hadn't occurred to me at the time, since she'd so rarely worn the circlet, to notice its absence. But she'd worn it that night. I myself had set the Heir's Circlet on her brow, coaxing her to wear it along with Salena's jewels. I'd never noted that the circlet hadn't been in the chest with the other jewels when I raided it to satisfy Illyria's demands a few days later.

Unreal that Uorsin had done that to her and no wonder she'd concealed it even from me. It had to have wounded her terribly—an injury that shadowed still behind her eyes. And Harlan had known all along. *They whisper for her execution, call her right to rule into question at court, and she cannot bring herself to deny their claims, overtly or to herself.*

How to salvage this? I had never been very good at telling lies, but if Ursula could not bring herself to do it, then I must. I owed it to both her and Salena. Goddesses take Uorsin for being such a rat bastard. For him I would wish the fate of being forever suspended in living death, ashes scattered to the winds.

"If I may, Your Highness?" I stood, gathering what little courage I possessed.

Ursula raised a brow at my unusual interruption, but I suspected she was grateful for it. No telling how she might have fielded this accusation, particularly as it seemed to be true. She was just honorable enough to abdicate after all, and we couldn't have that.

"Prince Stefan. Please accept my apologies for any confusion you may have suffered on this subject. The night of the announcement that Illyria would wed His Majesty King Uorsin, she requested the crown jewels as her due. I believe any number of people who were present can confirm." Especially as her "request" had been a horrifying demand, uttered over the beheaded body of the former chatelaine, who'd failed to provide an impromptu engagement feast to Illyria's liking. Several ambassadors nodded, more than one paling at the memory. "At Her Highness Ursula's command, I retrieved the jewels from her chambers and, in my haste and dismay, did not remove the circlet from the chest where it rested with the others. Please forgive me, Your Highness." I curtsied deeply to Ursula. "It was thoughtlessly done. I should be reprimanded for so carelessly relinquishing your Heir's Circlet to the enemy."

She considered me for a long moment. Long enough that I thought she might call me on the lie.

"Many of us had scattered thoughts that terrible night, Lady Mailloux," she finally said. "I think you can be forgiven. Especially as I retrieved the circlet myself from the imposter. Or rather, from her smoldering remains." She smiled in a grim satisfaction that turned out to be exactly the right note. People broke into cheers at the remembered triumph, the shouts ringing through the great hall. Ursula was heir, not only on paper, but by right of heroism. None could claim the same.

Stefan's smugness bled away like smoke from a doused candle.

~ 12 ~

I T WASN'T THE last of the political skirmishes, but in the wake of that particular earthquake, the rest proved to be minor ones. Not that there weren't dissenters and grumblers, but without Stefan's vocal leadership, no one else had the courage to speak up. Stefan wasn't happy, of course, and departed the next morning in a huff, announcing he refused to witness "that travesty of a coronation." He also refused to renew the treaty or give a vow of loyalty, but that mattered little. Such things fell to his father, King Teodor, regardless. As an additional blessing, he took the entirety of Duranor's armies with him—the final remnants of the looming civil war all had dreaded—declaring that Ordnung would have to defend itself without Duranor's help.

To Stefan's face, Ursula refrained from pointing out that such a statement was treasonous. Instead she had me transcribe a carefully worded missive to Teodor requesting his presence at the coronation, along with the tithe of troops he owed the High Throne, and incidentally mentioning that his son seemed to have mistakenly taken too many home and that she was sure he'd want to personally correct that oversight. The lethal gleam in her eye as she chose her words gave me a bit of a chill, knowing that's how she must look with the point of her sword at someone's throat. She refused all of my suggestions for mitigating the implicit accusation of treason.

"You're making an enemy of Stefan," I warned her, feeling I should.

"Not true," she corrected me, reading over the letter with a sharp-edged smile. "He was already my enemy. I'm just letting him know that I know it. I have no wish to follow in my father's tyrannical footsteps, but neither did Uorsin raise me to be too soft to hold the High Throne. You're determined to put me on it. I'm determined to stay there."

I breathed a mental sigh of relief at her resolute tone. Somewhere amidst the fighting for her right to rule, she'd given up some of the doubts that had plagued her.

Someone who knew her less well might have heard ambition in her words, or the lust for power, as Stefan assumed. I knew it for the duty she felt she owed her people. She might not be the megalomaniac her father had been, or someone like her mother, who'd acted because she believed only she could prevent a terrible possible future. No, Ursula was simply born for this. Salena had gone to impossible lengths to bring her daughter into being, blood of her blood, to hold and keep the peace. Danu's bright blade, avatar of justice that cut through the posturing and nonsense.

This is what made her a queen, while I remained the one who stood behind her.

AMBASSADORS, ROYALS OF all tiers, and various other representatives of lands far and near continued to arrive through the following weeks as word of the coronation continued to travel.

The sheer number of guests strained our hospitality with so little time to put the castle and environs to rights—or to replenish the supplies depleted by the siege situation Uorsin had created in his paranoia. Harlan finally convinced Ursula to delegate security to him, which let her concentrate on smoothing relationships. She didn't love ceding control of that aspect of things, but she trusted him to do it, which helped immensely.

Each daily onslaught of new arrivals, however, failed to produce the three guests I most hoped to greet. Zynda hadn't returned, but sent a vague message with the Tala artisans who delivered the new throne. I read it nine times, but never got more from it than I should be able to have what I wanted and they'd get to Ordnung eventually. As the goddess of the shapeshifters, of wild magic, the moon, and the ever-changing shadows of night, Moranu did not instill organization in her followers.

Conversely, the message sent from Danu's central temple, from a high peak at the nexus of six kingdoms, near the geographical center of the continent, had come back with crisp precision within days. They knew where to find the priestess I sought, but obliquely referenced that she must be retrieved, which would take some time. They also did not promise when she would arrive.

I began to kick myself for this brilliant plan. So far I not only lacked the perfect persons to crown Ursula—I had none at all. With Glorianna's central Temple on the grounds of Ordnung itself, I could have at least made that part easy, with so many convenient priests to choose from, most of them highly placed in the Church's hierarchy, but no. No, I had to send away to the White Monks, all the way on the coast of the Strait of K'van.

Who hadn't answered at all.

With a week until the coronation, I began to consider that I'd need a back-up plan. We had the throne and the crown. The rose window had been replaced with stained glass in three overlapping circles—Danu's star ascendant on a summer-blue field, Glorianna's sun against the pink of dawn or sunset on the lower right, and Moranu's crescent against a midnight sky on the left. Where the colors overlapped, they blended shades, so the curve-sided triangle in the center glowed a majestic purple. It was a thing of astonishing beauty.

Pennants once again flew from the shining towers of Ordnung—now thirteen of them, Annfwn's joining the others. Ursula's personal banner and the one Ami had designed to represent the united kingdoms were folded away, awaiting coronation day.

Ursula's sword had been repaired and she'd even, with surprisingly little rancor, met with Denise, the head seamstress, to discuss her coronation gown. Without me present. Which was fine, as I had more than enough to occupy me and Denise promised me that Ursula would look extraordinary. I tried not to be concerned when I heard she'd recruited the armorer for advice.

We were talking about Ursula, after all.

I'd very nearly decided to send to Danu's temple and ask them to send someone, anyone to perform the ceremony, when I got word that the person I'd most hoped to see had just been granted permission to enter Ordnung.

Ursula had adjourned court for the day and had gone for a "light workout" before the evening's meal. With more and more dignitaries in residence, the feasts grew longer and more elaborate with each passing day—with Ursula valiantly attempting not to count the cost of feeding so many so lavishly for so long. She deserved the outlet, so I kept my mouth shut when those supposedly light workouts produced bruises and the occasional bleeding wound.

At least those impressed the newer members of court, to witness for themselves the ferocity of their future High Queen—and would give them exciting tales to carry home. That she'd be in the practice yard for this reunion was serendipitous. A thrill of uncertainty went through me. Hopefully I had not overstepped.

I hurried to the inner courtyard, spotting our new visitor immediately. She'd grown older, of course, over the last dozen years. Goddesses knew we all had. But she also looked as supple and keen-edged as ever.

"Kaedrin!" I called out and her head whipped around to pick me out with unerring precision. She left her horse and strode to me, wrapping me in an enthusiastic embrace.

"Dafne." She squeezed my shoulders, scanning my face. No doubt witnessing the lines I'd gained. "Danu could have struck me down, I was so surprised to get your missive. Uorsin dead and our little Essla ready to take his place at last, eh?"

"Not so little. Wait until you see her. She's in the practice yard, naturally." We exchanged grins, turning together in that direction. "Will you do it—handle Danu's part of the ceremony? You're still a priestess?"

"Once a priestess of Danu, always one," she averred. "And it will be the greatest honor of my life. You know how I hated to leave her to him."

"Yes." Ursula had been desolate for months after Uorsin banished her mentor—along with all mentions of Danu and Moranu—from Ordnung. "But you equipped her well. Look."

We stopped just inside the practice yard, the snow of the morning's storm melted away from the sun-warmed stones.

Ursula sparred with Harlan, while some of the other Hawks and Vervaldr watched and others ran their own exercises. Lean and lithe as the daggers she used, Ursula spun in and out of Harlan's brutal attack, avoiding the devastating sweeps of his broadsword, wielded with all the brute strength of his large body. I winced, unable to look, knowing now where the bruises came from.

Neither of them ever held back. And she looked less strained than she had an hour before, now fierce and free, bleeding off the tension of the days. Something else he did for her.

Kaedrin waited until Ursula, laughing, danced back from a narrow miss. "You're still dropping your left guard," she called out.

Ursula, never taken by surprise, froze in shock. Then turned.

"Kaedrin?" She whispered it, staring as if at an apparition.

Kaedrin held out her palms and shrugged. "That or the avatar of Danu come to discuss your failures of discipline."

Shaking her head, Ursula handed her daggers hilt-first to Harlan, then broke into a run and seized her old mentor in a fierce embrace. "I never thought I'd see you again." Her gray eyes, not steely at all, but fogged with uncharacteristic tears, found me where I hovered on the edges still. *Thank you*, she mouthed. And I knew it had been the right decision.

AFTER KAEDRIN'S ARRIVAL, as if Danu's blessing had created the path, everything else fell into place. Andi and Rayfe returned to Ordnung, bringing word that Zynda would arrive shortly with the same shaman who'd married them. He'd been on some sort of retreat somewhere in the depths of Annfwn, but had been persuaded to leave his homeland. Andi promised he and Zynda would be in time. I made a deliberate resolution to believe her. I also managed not to ask again about the Dasnarians. She'd said she'd tell me if anything changed.

Apparently we still had time.

Ami and Ash also returned with the twins in tow—both babies seeming as if they'd grown a hand's-length each. And both, it turned out, had shapeshifted during their time at Castle Avonlidgh. Stella had led the way, becoming a black jaguar kitten—something that seemed to please Andi no end—and Astar, upon witnessing the event, had crawled after her, transforming into a baby bear, swiping at her escapades.

They recounted the tale over a private dinner, a great relief after all the formal feasts and one they insisted I join, despite that I made for an uneven seventh at the table. By the time Ami told it, from the mad escape from the nursery, to the consternation of the castle guard and Ash's eventual rescue of the spitting kitten from the height of one of the tapestries—heroics for which he bore four long scratches on his forearm that he claimed he wouldn't part with even if he could heal himself— everyone was in tears from laughter. Ursula even took Harlan's hand, lacing her fingers with his and exchanging a long look, as if at some private joke.

"I'm just glad you thought to send those Tala nurses with us," Ami told Andi, wiping the moisture from under her eyes. "I don't know *what* we would have done otherwise."

"I'm glad, too," Andi said, "though I didn't really expect them to shift so soon."

"Especially so far from Annfwn," Rayfe put in, frowning a little.

Ash shook his head, going solemn. "I'll tell you—what we'd heard doesn't touch on the reality. The magic eddying around the countryside, it comes in fits and starts, sometimes crashing like surf and then leaving only tide pools behind. In some places it's much stronger than anywhere I encountered inside Annfwn. In others, it's almost barren."

That sobered everyone. "And Windroven?" Ursula asked Ami.

"Rumbling," she confirmed. "But so far no more than that. We're watching it and we've made evacuation plans."

"It will be full winter soon."

"I know that," Ami retorted. "I've been snowed in at Windroven, but Glorianna curse me if I'm going to make everyone leave during late fall harvest just for some rumbling."

Ursula rapped her knuckles on the table, jaw tightening "Yes, but how long do we get between rumbling and exploding?"

"I don't know!" Ami fired back. "We haven't done volcanoes before."

"Unless you count within the family," Andi remarked to Rayfe in a dry tone.

Ami ignored her. "These are *my* people, too. *My* home. Let me handle it, Essla."

Harlan refilled Ursula's wine goblet and nudged it against her clenched fist. She flicked him a glance and uncurled her fingers in a deliberate move. "You're right." Then she grinned. "But if my niece and nephew shapeshift in Ordnung, you get to handle that, too. *I* won't be chasing any jaguar kittens."

Ami groaned and dropped her forehead onto the table, Ash stroking her hair in amused comfort.

I made a note to study up on volcanoes.

~ 13 ~

THE WHITE MONK arrived the following day, two days before coronation.

He arrived so inauspiciously that I wasn't notified as I had been with Kaedrin. I'd cut through the arcade on my way back from leaving some texts in Ursula's rooms that she'd asked for, when I encountered the white-robed and hooded man standing, arms folded into his sleeves in a small courtyard. Not the one Ursula liked to use for private workouts, but one just down from that, attached to the family wing. He seemed to be staring at the grass. Dry autumn leaves whirled in a chilly breeze, chuckling in hoarse whispers as they brushed the stone walls. The urns had been emptied of flowers following the first frost, but for some reason the patch of grass remained green.

Perhaps that's why he stared.

I cleared my throat. He didn't move.

"Excuse me," I said.

"I know you're there, Lady Mailloux," he replied, his voice a softer scratch than the leaves, the voice of a man who seldom speaks. "So this is where they did it."

Was it? I hadn't known. Though it made sense, given the relative privacy of the place. I shivered, abruptly cold without my cloak. The arcade would have to be closed for the winter soon.

"Thank you for coming to Ordnung." I stepped closer.

"It's not a small thing," he said, still not looking at me, "to sacrifice a king to the land. Tell me. Did all three daughters have a hand in it?"

"As I understand it. I wasn't present."

He glanced at me then, icy blue eyes the only color in a pale face, lined with age. "No. You wouldn't have been. Your sacrifice is still coming, isn't it?"

I began to understand why Ursula complained about vague prophecies. "I think you're mistaken. I'm only a librarian—now councilor to the future High Queen. I asked you here to participate in her coronation, as a representative of Glorianna."

He only gave me a slow nod of confirmation that I'd spoken the obvious.

"How shall I address you?" I tried.

"I am the White Monk."

Exactly as Ash used to say. I nearly smiled at the memory of Ami stomping her foot and screeching, "That's a title, not a name!"

As if I'd called him with the memory, Ash came striding through the arcade, then stopped in his tracks. The old man turned to him and made the circle of Glorianna. Ash bowed deeply, then approached the monk and knelt, bowing his head, and the man laid his hands upon it. All in silence.

Feeling like an intruder on something sacred that did not belong to me, I slipped away. But not before the monk caught my eye, and winked.

THE MORNING OF the coronation found me in Ursula's rooms as

the ladies dressed her for the ceremony. Zynda would arrive with the priest of Moranu at any moment, Andi had assured me. *Goddesses make it so.* Ursula didn't need my help, but I had taken over her desk, fielding last-minute emergencies, mostly via notes and pages running frantically about. I occasionally needed her to weigh in on a decision. It was easier, I justified to myself, to remain with her.

Mostly, I wouldn't have missed seeing the assembly of this gown for anything.

The ladies I'd assigned to her bustled about happily, enjoying their rare opportunity to primp their future High Queen for what might be the only coronation they'd see in their lifetimes, *Goddesses willing.* For her part, Ursula showed more patience than I'd expected for the extensive preparation it took to make her concept work. Of course, she'd confided, a month of ceaseless politics, ruffled feather-smoothing and negotiating made her grateful for *any* respite.

I agreed with her, nursing a secret plan to slip out of the celebration ball early, crawl under the covers of my bed and sleep for days. It wouldn't happen, but the fantasy kept me going.

"One point of troubling news," I told her, "is that Prince Cavan of Erie and his bride, Princess Nix, late of the Remus Isles have arrived."

Ursula raised an eyebrow. "Did Uorsin know about that alliance?"

"I believe King Wyn kept that information quiet. Old Queen Isyn, Nix's mother, yet lives—but once she passes it appears that both Erie and Remus will fall under Cavan's rule."

Harlan, observing the proceedings from a chair by the fire, frowned. The weather had grown decidedly chill, though the sun shone brightly enough to satisfy those who worried over omens. It surprised me a bit, that he elected to stay for the primping, but something about the way he kept an eye on Ursula made me think he had good reason. Whatever significance the gown held for her, he understood and was careful of it. "Remus is not one of the Twelve, correct?"

Ursula flicked him a glance in the full-length mirror Ami had sent over from her rooms. "No. It's a chain of islands, very insular people. Rumors of magic even wilder than we've seen."

"Apparently quite a bit magical has happened there as well in the last month or so," I told her. "And we'll have to discuss how *that* alliance will affect things."

"Put meeting with them on the schedule for tomorrow then."

As if said schedule wasn't already overloaded, but I made a note.

The ladies had so far fastened her into a corset over a light shift, which Ursula accepted with reasonable grace as they insisted it would be necessary to support the gown. Denise had tackled the challenge of creating the unusual gown with enthusiastic determination—along with the extensive and unprecedented collaboration with the armorer—using steel boning inside the stiff fabric of the corset.

"Being able to breathe would be helpful," Ursula commented wryly as they tightened the laces.

"Believe me, Your Highness," Denise replied, surveying her work and nodding at Ursula in the mirror, "you'll be grateful for the back support before this day is done. This is not an inconsiderable amount of weight to carry. Think of it as a kind of armor."

"A bulwark against protocol?" Ursula huffed out a pained

laugh.

To my gut-clenching relief, an out-of-breath page arrived with a note from the gates that said Zynda had arrived. Minutes later, the Tala woman knocked and was admitted. She came in, dusty from the roads, but also radiant and tanned from Annfwn's sun, bringing the scent of wintery air and tropical flowers with her. Halting, she scanned the elaborate skeleton of the supports for Ursula's gown, whistling in amazement.

"*So* not how the Tala do it," she remarked.

Ursula frowned at her in the mirror. "Blame Dafne. She insisted on all this pomp and ceremony."

"You picked the gown," I reminded her. It hardly seemed possible all would be done by day's end. "Did you…" I started to ask Zynda, then broke off in panic at what I'd do if she gave me the wrong answer.

She grinned easily. "Moranu's shaman is here. He's consulting with the White Monk and the Priestess of Danu in the small family courtyard. Kaedrin asks you meet them there, when you're available, to discuss details."

Interesting that they picked that spot. "Thank you," I told her, fervently. "I'll be right down."

"No need to hurry, I think."

"But they don't speak Tala and he speaks nothing but. I should go translate."

"They seemed to have a plan. I wouldn't worry." She patted my shoulder, wholly unaware of how much could still go wrong, and nodded to Ursula. "I'm glad we made it back in time. I must go bathe and change."

"You don't need to be present," Ursula told her. "Aren't you tired from the journey?"

Zynda's grin lightened her face. "A bit, but I wouldn't miss seeing my cousin crowned High Queen for anything in the world. Salena would come back and haunt me for it!"

Zynda turned with a jaunty wave, missing the strange expression that crossed Ursula's face, the way she touched a hand to her stomach. She left again, singing a song I recalled Zyr had liked. It felt like forever ago since that going away party. The ladies finished strapping on the metal kirtle needed to support the heavy skirts of the gown.

"I feel like I'm in one of those cages the ladies keep their birds in," Ursula remarked. "As I can barely breathe, don't be surprised if I make whistling noises."

"This was your idea," I said again, to save Denise having to. Though I'd been dubious about Ursula's concept, and whether it could be done in time—or at all—I had to admit that, as they added the final layers, it was an extraordinary accomplishment.

The ladies added first the petticoats over the metal kirtle, then the red velvet undergown in pieces. The bodice followed.

Then the actual gown on top of it all.

Made from polished silver chain mail from the armory, the skirts required three ladies to lift and hold them in place as they attached them with sturdy hooks to the boning of the corset. Denise fitted the bodice over the top, using silver ribbons to secure it, then stepped back to study the effect.

The gown fell as any dress would, from the high neck to the narrow waist, then flaring out to mimic cloth skirts, but constructed entirely of metal. The armorer had created it according to the lines Denise gave him and he'd outdone himself. The final result looked as if she wore armor shaped as a gown. The armorer had even been able to create a golden sheath affixed to the waist and skirt so she could wear her sword.

Ursula tested the grip. "It's not exactly the right angle for my best speed."

"If you have to draw your sword today," I said, "we have bigger problems than that."

She flicked me a glance and didn't reply, but Harlan snorted softly.

The rubies at her breast and wrists, set in gold, matches to the one in the pommel of her sword, caught the color of her hair and the undergown. Her eyes glinted as silver as the sparkling links, striking exactly the right note.

She was magnificent.

The ladies oohed, put the last touches on her hair and the subtle makeup Ursula had agreed to, and bowed out to take their places in the hall. Ursula remained still for a moment longer, a somber expression on her face as she studied herself in the mirror, making me wonder what she saw there.

"Nervous?" Harlan asked her, before I could, which meant he earned the glare instead.

"I'm having a big piece of jewelry stuck on my head," she retorted. "What's to be nervous about?"

He stood, surveying her, then gave her a hand to step down from the pedestal they'd had her on, and some of her tension melted at his touch. Though the toes of her silver heeled boots showed under the shorter hem at the front, the back dragged heavily on the floor, making a soft gravelly noise, like the amplified sound of a snake sliding through grass or over sand. A dramatic effect, but…

"Does it weigh too much?" I asked her.

"I won't be sprinting in it, Danu knows. If you wish me to be painted in it, you'd best hire a fast artist."

"But can you dance in it?"

"I will not be dancing," she said in a firm tone. "I shall sit on my new throne and oversee the dancing and that's final. Hopefully no one will try to attack me as I'd be a sitting duck even if I could draw fast enough."

Harlan grinned at her. "Then I shall have to stand at the ready to defend my lady fair."

"Ha-ha. More likely I'll need those muscles to lever me up off the floor if I topple over. That would scandalize the court, their High Queen stranded on her back like a turtle."

"You look magnificent," Harlan echoed my thoughts. "The chain-mail gown is the perfect choice. Is it like enough to your vision?"

What vision? Her lips trembled a bit as she smiled at him. Tears pricked my own eyes. To compose myself and give them the illusion of privacy, I checked the crown. It also was a fine choice, much simpler than Uorsin's had been, a broader gold band than the circlet, that swelled to an upward point over her forehead, set with three of Salena's rubies in a staggered line, to represent the three goddesses, the topmost cut to resemble Danu's star.

"Close enough," she answered him. "And all the better that *this* one does not paralyze me."

"And you're not alone," he said. "You changed the story."

"I think you did. I wouldn't be standing here today without you."

They were quiet. If I could have, I'd have vanished myself from the room. Finally Harlan said, "It's the perfect symbol. Salena would approve—and be very proud of you at this moment."

"Thank you," she whispered. "For everything."

Satisfied the crown had no smudges and that Ursula would have composed herself, I closed the lid. "Ready?"

They looked good together, Harlan also in matching chain mail, with a crimson velvet shirt beneath that matched the rubies. Just as well the banner Ami designed had been also done in gold, silver and ruby red: a hawk stooping—though its talons clutched a strand of ivy, the symbol for peace—with a sun and crescent moon on either side, Danu's star at the peak. It lay ready to ascend Ordnung's heights as the coronation was completed.

I didn't expect the overwhelming swell of sentiment. As long as I'd dreamed of this day, I hadn't expected to feel like this, as if everything had truly come together, shimmering like the harmony of gold and silver together. A shining omen of a good future for us all, one of peace and prosperity.

"Yes." Ursula touched the hilt of her sword and squared her shoulders. "Let's get this over with so we can get back to doing something useful. Like breathing."

It felt good to laugh. Good to enjoy this feeling for as long as it lasted.

~ 14 ~

A S PROMISED, I found the White Monk, Kaedrin, and the Tala shaman gathered in the small grassy courtyard. They should have seemed like an odd grouping—the pale, ancient man in his white robes; the warrior woman, dressed in silver armor so bright it hurt the eyes; and the fur-clad shaman, dark hair falling in knotted ropes around his shoulders, braided with bits of colorful rags and beads. The three stood in a circle around the unseasonably green grass, eyes closed in prayer or silent communion.

Kaedrin opened her eyes at my approach, senses as acute as Ursula's. "This is good," she intoned, sounding not at all like herself. Her eyes burned bright as her armor and I felt as if Danu herself studied me. The shaman turned also, deep blue eyes so dark as to be midnight, Moranu's shadows in them. The White Monk smiled at me with Glorianna's infinite love.

"You can leave the ceremony to us," Kaedrin said. "We are ready."

As one, they inscribed the symbols of their goddesses in the air over the living grass, Glorianna's circle, Moranu's crescent, Danu's sword. Then they turned and walked side-by-side toward the great hall.

So much for discussing details.

I lingered a moment longer, taking a calming breath after looking into the gazes of three goddesses. Feeling the reverence of the moment, I offered up a prayer, as I seldom did. Then drew a circle in the air, cut by the crescent, bisected by the sword.

For a moment I imagined I felt Salena's cool hand on my brow. A murmur of her voice in my ear, that day coming back so vividly, the red-faced baby girl in my arms.

"You're holding the future High Queen, Dafne. I won't be there, but you will. I'm trusting her to you."

"Thank you, Salena," I whispered to the air. "You are remembered this day."

I went in and took the side door, to come in behind the great throne that now stood alone at the head of the hall, facing the new window high over the entrance. Taking the crown from its box, I set it on the seat of the throne and stepped back to observe. Everyone who'd been able to had assembled, the hall as full as I'd ever seen it. So much so that the center aisle barely stood free enough for passage.

My vantage point, behind and off to the side, let me scan all the faces. All had broken out their finest clothing and jewels, making the occasion the grandest of any I'd seen, including Ami and Hugh's wedding. In the forefront stood the highest representatives of most of the Thirteen Kingdoms, some royal, some not. I almost didn't recognize Ambassador Laurenne in her cloth of gold gown and the elaborate traditional headdress of Aerron. King Teodor flanked her, meeting my gaze with a grave nod. Good for him. On his other side, stood the young future king and queen of Erie and Remus, Cavan and Nix. They looked like bookends, she as fair as he was dark. Did all the denizens of Remus share that coloring? With her pale blue eyes, winter-white skin and ivory hair, she looked to be carved from ice. Except for the pink blush when Cavan smiled at her.

As we'd agreed, Ami and Andi stood on either side of the center aisle, both wearing Salena's rubies. Rayfe, who I'd never seen dressed so formally, stood beside Andi, both of them dressed in the bloodred of Tala royalty. Ash ranged a few spaces back from Ami, wearing the white robes of his order. Ami hadn't liked it, but agreed to the protocol, wearing the purple and green of Avonlidgh. Lady Veronica of Lianore, who'd saved us once on the journey to Windroven, accompanied Ami, arm in arm with one of the Vervaldr. Her eyes sparkled with great excitement.

I'd been dubious about the wisdom of it—and the potential debacle—but Astar and Stella played at Ami's feet. Stella with her wild dark curls wore a tiny version of Andi's bloodred velvet, the image of both her aunt and of her Grandmother Salena. Astar, her fair mirror, in the colors of Avonlidgh. He gazed about at the spectacle with wide blue eyes the color of the summer sky and I caught my breath, seeing Hugh so strongly in him.

All of our ghosts, present and accounted for.

A hush fell over the room and the great doors opened, spilling noonday light through, to add to the colors scattered by the window of the Goddesses. It splintered off Ursula, scattering diamonds of light like stars, and a sigh ran through the assembly.

She moved slowly down the center aisle, head held nobly high. Harlan followed, her personal guard, forever at her back.

No one had even tried to argue about that.

As she passed, like a wave, the people bowed to her. The guard along the walls bent their heads with respect and reverence. No one could fail to be moved by the sight. Even the faces of her detractors held awe. They'd no doubt be back to squabbling as soon as tomorrow, but at this sacred noon, peace united us all.

Perhaps Salena had seen this key image. I hoped so.

The three celebrants stepped up to form a triangle before the throne, Kaedrin at the center, flanked by the White Monk and the Tala shaman. Ursula stopped before them and inclined her head.

The Tala shaman spoke to Andi and she answered the summons. She held still and calm as he turned over her hand, placed a black feather in her palm. One, I felt certain, that came from Rayfe's bird form. Then he used a large blade to cut her wrist. I'd held her hand long ago when he'd done the same at her wedding, binding her with blood to Rayfe. She hadn't flinched either time.

Magic filled the air, heavy and prescient.

The White Monk beckoned Ami to step forward, taking her hand in his, then filling her palm with pink rose petals. Kaedrin handed him a small dagger and poised it over her delicate wrist. She glanced back at Ash, who gave her a slow nod. Echoing it, she said something I couldn't hear to the White Monk, then winced as he cut her wrist in a shallow swipe, holding it so her bright blood flowed over the petals, reddening them.

Kaedrin asked Ursula for her sword, which she drew fast enough to my eye, then told her to hold up her hands. With exquisite skill, she used the tip to score Ursula's palms, opening twin wells of blood. Taking the stained rose petals from Ami, Kaedrin filled Ursula's right palm with them. Then she placed the feather from Andi, now crimson with her blood, into Ursula's left hand.

Holding the sword hilt wrapped in both hands, pointing

straight to the sun, high overhead, Kaedrin spoke.

"Child of Danu, she of the bright blade and the clear eyes, you come before these people to right the wrongs of the past. This is no honor the goddesses bestow upon you, but the gravest onus. The paths of blood, of family, of training, and duty have brought you to this moment, but now the decision rests with you. The mantle of responsibility that awaits you will weigh heavier than any armor. Will you take it upon you, knowing that no power, no ambition, no worldly wealth will ever balance its weight? The eyes of your people rest on you, their blood on your hands. Will you take up your sword to protect them? Will you clasp the sword that Danu gives you, seal it with the mercy of Glorianna and the sorcery of Moranu? Will you bind them, as you bind the kingdoms who will look to you forever more, for protection, for guidance, for the love that is Glorianna's, for the life-giving magic that is Moranu's, and for the unflinching justice that is Danu's?"

Ursula's eyes, clear steel as the sword before her, met Kaedrin's. She didn't hesitate.

"I will."

Kaedrin lowered the hilt between Ursula's palms, wrapping her hands around the High Queen's as she clasped the blood, petals and feather to the shining metal.

"I give you Danu's blessing, to reign, to protect your realm and dispense justice in her name."

The White Monk set back his hood and put his hand on Ursula's right shoulder. He said nothing, but the love and serenity in his smile spoke everything. The shaman did likewise, clasping Ursula's left shoulder, saying in Tala, "Through my hand to your blood, Moranu speaks, giving life and magic to the lands you watch over, forever more."

They held the moment the air shimmering with numinous presence.

Kaedrin looked to me. "The crown, librarian."

I nearly didn't move, so stunned was I. Their plan had not accounted for getting the crown onto the High Queen? Aware of the weight of the moment, I tried to move gracefully, taking up the crown without smudging it and carrying it to Kaedrin. Though her face remained solemn, the aura of Danu about her still, her gaze held amusement.

"The goddesses bless you," she said, her voice carrying. "But the law sets the crown upon your head. Accept this symbol of your rule from your chosen councilor, as you will also forever accept her counsel."

My heart nearly stopped, sweating fingers slipping on the polished metal. This was *not* the plan. Ursula's silver-edged gaze found mine, narrow lips curving into a smile at my expense. "I so accept the wisdom of history and the knowledge of law from my chosen councilor."

Nothing for it but to do it. I stepped forward, totally unsure how I'd reach. Not through the tangle of arms and the sword, certainly. I moved behind Ursula and Harlan dropped to one knee, offering a hand. All right then. I stepped onto the platform of his thigh, unutterably grateful that he steadied me by the hips. With utmost care, I set the crown on Ursula's head, settling it there as I'd done with her circlet only months before.

It should have been absurd and yet, it all felt exactly right. It was done.

Salena's voice murmured in my memory.

Perfect.

EPILOGUE

I STEPPED OUTSIDE the ballroom onto a balcony, in need of air and a quiet moment to myself.

Ordnung blazed with light as I'd never seen it. The walls glowed white even in the dark of night, lit by thousands of torches. Everywhere music and shouts of joy rang out.

High on the towers, Ursula's banner flew proudly, along with the newest, for all Thirteen Kingdoms. The thirteen interlinked rings formed a chain within the three overlapping circles of the goddesses. A fine companion to Ursula's hawk and a flag that would, Goddesses willing, outlast us all. Never mind that the Remus Isles would make for fourteen. Perhaps we needed to think of a name that wouldn't include numbers.

"Had enough dancing?" Zynda leaned on the railing next to me.

"And then some," I replied. "I haven't danced this much since…" My going away party in Annfwn.

Zynda tossed back her long hair, damp with sweat at her temples. "Anyone special?"

"Dance partners? Goddesses no." Though it seemed a fair number of men who hadn't known my name before today had become quite friendly. The price of a suddenly high profile.

"Zyr said hello, by the way, and I'm to ask if you've changed your mind. Something going on between you two I should know?"

"No," I said, a little too fast. Making her raise her brows in question. "I mean—he's not for me. A lovely man, to be sure, but I really don't think that—"

Zynda held up a hand, laughing. "You don't have to fall over yourself to explain."

But I remembered that night. That kiss. A song not meant for me, but maybe somewhere out there... *Maybe you need to do less waiting and more wandering.* No. That was foolish sentimentality. Maybe a bit of let-down after so much planning and excitement. My place was in Ordnung, with the High Queen. It would be enough.

I hadn't forgotten Andi's vision, of Dasnarians in our future. I would be far too busy for frivolities like dancing or kissing handsome men. Certainly no wandering. With trials ahead of us, I might look back and be grateful to have had the energy to feel restless.

No one can take away the dances you've already had.

"On second thought, I haven't had enough dancing."

"It's a pity to miss a party—even one that isn't yours," Zynda agreed.

But it was mine, in a way. The day may have been full of ghosts, but I still lived. "Yes. Let's go celebrate."

Dafne's story continues in
THE PAGES OF THE MIND

TITLES BY JEFFE KENNEDY

OTHER FANTASY ROMANCES

A COVENANT OF THORNS

Rogue's Pawn
Rogue's Possession
Rogue's Paradise

THE TWELVE KINGDOMS

Negotiation
The Mark of the Tala
The Tears of the Rose
The Talon of the Hawk
Heart's Blood
The Crown of the Queen

THE UNCHARTED REALMS

The Pages of the Mind
The Edge of the Blade
The Snows of Windroven
The Shift of the Tide
The Arrows of the Heart
The Dragons of Summer
The Fate of the Tala

THE CHRONICLES OF DASNARIA

Prisoner of the Crown
Exile of the Seas
Warrior of the World

SORCEROUS MOONS

Lonen's War
Oria's Gambit
The Tides of Bára
The Forests of Dru
Oria's Enchantment
Lonen's Reign

THE FORGOTTEN EMPIRES

The Orchid Throne
The Fiery Crown

CONTEMPORARY ROMANCES

Shooting Star

MISSED CONNECTIONS

Last Dance
With a Prince
Since Last Christmas

CONTEMPORARY EROTIC ROMANCES

Exact Warm Unholy
The Devil's Doorbell

FACETS OF PASSION

Sapphire
Platinum

Ruby
Five Golden Rings

FALLING UNDER

Going Under
Under His Touch
Under Contract

EROTIC PARANORMAL

MASTER OF THE OPERA E-SERIAL

Master of the Opera, Act 1: Passionate Overture
Master of the Opera, Act 2: Ghost Aria
Master of the Opera, Act 3: Phantom Serenade
Master of the Opera, Act 4: Dark Interlude
Master of the Opera, Act 5: A Haunting Duet
Master of the Opera, Act 6: Crescendo
Master of the Opera

BLOOD CURRENCY

Blood Currency

BDSM FAIRYTALE ROMANCE

Petals and Thorns

OTHER WORKS

Birdwoman
Hopeful Monsters
Teeth, Long and Sharp

Thank you for reading!

About Jeffe Kennedy

Jeffe Kennedy is an award-winning author whose works include novels, non-fiction, poetry, and short fiction. She has won the prestigious RITA® Award from Romance Writers of America (RWA), has been a finalist twice, been a Ucross Foundation Fellow, received the Wyoming Arts Council Fellowship for Poetry, and was awarded a Frank Nelson Doubleday Memorial Award. She serves on the Board of Directors for the Science Fiction and Fantasy Writers of America (SFWA) as a Director at Large.

Her award-winning fantasy romance trilogy *The Twelve Kingdoms* hit the shelves starting in May 2014. Book 1, *The Mark of the Tala*, received a starred Library Journal review and was nominated for the RT Book of the Year while the sequel, *The Tears of the Rose* received a Top Pick Gold and was nominated for the RT Reviewers' Choice Best Fantasy Romance of 2014. The third book, *The Talon of the Hawk*, won the RT Reviewers' Choice Best Fantasy Romance of 2015. Two more books followed in this world, beginning the spin-off series *The Uncharted Realms*. Book one in that series, *The Pages of the Mind*, was nominated for the RT Reviewer's Choice Best Fantasy Romance of 2016 and won RWA's 2017 RITA Award. The second book, *The Edge of the Blade*, released December 27, 2016, and was a PRISM finalist, along with *The Pages of the Mind*. The next in the series, *The Shift of the Tide* and *The Arrows of the Heart* came out in August, 2017, and October, 2018. A high fantasy trilogy, The Chronicles of Dasnaria, taking place in *The Twelve Kingdoms* world began releasing from Rebel Base books in 2018. The novella, *The*

Dragons of Summer, first appearing in the *Seasons of Sorcery* anthology, finaled for the 2019 RITA Award.

She also introduced a new fantasy romance series, *Sorcerous Moons*, which includes *Lonen's War*, *Oria's Gambit*, *The Tides of Bàra*, *The Forests of Dru*, *Oria's* Enchantment, *and Lonen's Reign*. She's begun releasing a new contemporary erotic romance series, *Missed Connections*, which started with *Last Dance* and continues in *With a Prince* and *Since Last Christmas*.

In September 2019, St. Martins Press released *The Orchid Throne*, the first book in a new romantic fantasy series, *The Forgotten Empires*. The sequel, *The Fiery Crown*, will follow in May 2021.

Her other works include a number of fiction series: the fantasy romance novels of *A Covenant of Thorns*; the contemporary BDSM novellas of the *Facets of Passion*; an erotic contemporary serial novel, *Master of the Opera*; and the erotic romance trilogy, *Falling Under*, which includes *Going Under*, *Under His Touch* and *Under Contract*.

She lives in Santa Fe, New Mexico, with two Maine coon cats, plentiful free-range lizards and a very handsome Doctor of Oriental Medicine.

Jeffe can be found online at her website: JeffeKennedy.com, every Sunday at the popular SFF Seven blog, on Facebook, on Goodreads and pretty much constantly on Twitter @jeffekennedy. She is represented by Sarah Younger of Nancy Yost Literary Agency.

jeffekennedy.com

facebook.com/Author.Jeffe.Kennedy

twitter.com/jeffekennedy

goodreads.com/author/show/1014374.Jeffe_Kennedy

Sign up for her newsletter here.

jeffekennedy.com/sign-up-for-my-newsletter